Ten minutes past one

With her eyes wide open, Gail lay stiffly in the bed. She could hear a faint rustling of branches outside the window and the scraping of a piece of metal on the roof. The wind must have come up, she reasoned. If she'd been up in her own room, she would easily have sorted out the sounds, knowing which were usual in the settling old house and identifying any strange ones, but being in an isolated room at the back of the house gave her a different perspective.

She waited uneasily.

A loud thud echoed through the house. Gail was confused as to where the noise had come from. Upstairs or somewhere on the ground floor? She couldn't tell. She waited. Another muffled sound reached her ears. All doubt fled.

Someone was in the house.

ABOUT THE AUTHOR

Leona Karr's favorite genre for reading and writing has always been romantic suspense. Every bookcase is filled with exciting offerings, both new and old. Many of her more than twenty published novels, including *Flashpoint,* are set against the exciting backdrop of the Colorado Rocky Mountains where she makes her home. She lives in Denver with her husband, Marshall.

Books by Leona Karr

HARLEQUIN INTRIGUE

Flashpoint

Leona Karr

Harlequin Books

TORONTO • NEW YORK • LONDON
AMSTERDAM • PARIS • SYDNEY • HAMBURG
STOCKHOLM • ATHENS • TOKYO • MILAN
MADRID • WARSAW • BUDAPEST • AUCKLAND

To my agent, Adele Leone, with deep thanks for
ten years of guidance, loyalty and friendship

Harlequin Intrigue edition published May 1993

ISBN 0-373-22227-0

FLASHPOINT

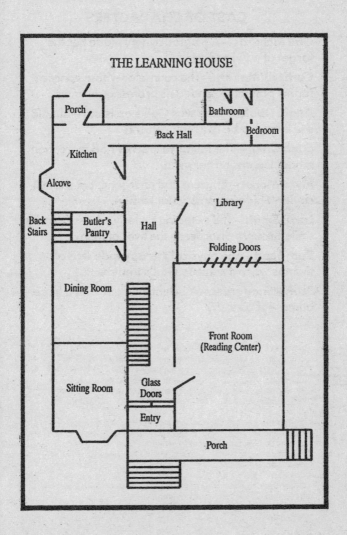

THE LEARNING HOUSE

Porch

Bathroom

Bedroom

Back Hall

Kitchen

Alcove

Library

Back Stairs

Butler's Pantry

Hall

Folding Doors

Dining Room

Front Room (Reading Center)

Sitting Room

Glass Doors

Entry

Porch

CAST OF CHARACTERS

Gail Richards—A tragic accident made her the target of a twisted mind.

Curtis O'Mallory—The counselor whose concern for his patient exceeded its professional limits.

Angie Difalco—She was Gail's assistant—but did she intend to be her replacement?

Edith Crum—The talkative teacher had more than school lessons on her mind.

Myra Monet—Efficient and energetic, but she still couldn't hide her emotional tension.

Larry Smith—The outgoing orderly whose friendly smile brought disorder to the lives of many.

Beth Scott—The physical therapy aide was all thumbs when it came to Gail's treatment.

Scuffy Snodgrass—A bright little girl with a huge bump—of curiosity.

Prologue

The woman sat alone, unobtrusive and distant, in her usual corner of the small café. The clatter of trays, dishes and the relentless hum of voices around her failed to penetrate her concentration as she read the morning edition of the *Denver Post*. On page three, an account of a fatal automobile accident caught her attention. As she read the story, sweat beaded on her brow, her stomach muscles began to knot, her breath quickened and the familiar slither of an uncontrollable serpent twisted her insides, coiled ready to spring. Ugly. Demanding.

Holding the newspaper up in front of her face, she hid her tortured expression from people sitting at the nearest table a few feet away. She bit down on her lower lip as the words flew off the page, stabbing her like poisoned stilettos.

No, she pleaded silently. *Not again.* She wouldn't give in. Not this time. She wouldn't read any more about the woman who had lost control of her car on an icy hill and slid into another vehicle, killing a teenage boy. She struggled to subdue the uncontrollable demon that tortured and commanded her, but an un-

appeased rage grew, swelling inside her. She closed her
eyes as the woman's name vibrated in her head. *Gail
Richards*.

The sound of laughter at a nearby table brought a
burst of fury into the woman's heated face. No one
cared. No one would see that justice was done. *Gail
Richards...Gail Richards*. The name fixed itself in her
memory. Another murderer...just like the driver who
had run a stop sign and killed Robbie. Pain drilled into
her temples. She wanted to claw at the roots of her hair
and dig her nails into her own flesh, but she knew it
wouldn't do any good.

Only one thing would help. Gail Richards had to
pay...just like the man who had killed his own child
while driving drunk and the teenage girl who had
backed over an innocent two-year-old boy. They had
paid for their crimes. The serpent inside her had been
appeased but now it coiled within her again. Only
justice would assuage her torment.

It's all right, Robbie. Mother won't forget. The
woman laid down her newspaper. Her lips moved.
"Gail Richards." The whispered name was like an
ugly promise.

Chapter One

Nearly four weeks after the accident, Gail Richards returned home to a Victorian mansion set back from a street in east Denver. Its rambling veranda, numerous cupolas and gingerbread bargeboards were reminiscent of an old dowager who had seen better days but retained her dignity in the midst of encroaching high-rise apartments only a couple of blocks away.

Gail had inherited the old house from an aunt a year ago. At first Gail didn't see how she could maintain it on her teacher's salary but she hated to sell the vintage home. Searching for a means to keep the property, Gail visited some private, profit-making teaching academies, and decided she might be able to keep the mansion by turning the lower floor into a learning center where she could offer diagnostic testing and private reading instruction. Even though she had graduated from the University of Colorado as a reading specialist, she had always been assigned to a regular classroom. The idea of having her own reading center excited her.

The idea had proved to be viable. After only eight months, Gail had been pleased with both the financial and professional results. Most of her enrollment consisted of students who were not doing well in school, but she also had a number of illiterate adults who wanted to learn to read.

She had her private living quarters on the second floor—at least that had been the arrangement until a car accident a month ago. Now, she planned to use a room that had once been the servants' quarters behind the kitchen since she would be hobbling around with a cane for a few more weeks.

"I just don't understand how such a thing could have happened," said Angie Difalco when she brought Gail home from the hospital. The teacher's assistant shook her curly dark head as they approached the front steps. "You're one of the best drivers I know, Gail. And to think the rest of us just went on having a good time at the party... not even knowing you'd rammed into that car and injured your back. Such a tragedy. That poor teenager killed and you nearly paralyzed for life." She sighed. "Sometimes the best of drivers—"

"I told you—someone hit me from behind and shoved my Volvo across the intersection into the other car."

Angie's round face took a humoring expression. "Yes, yes. And it's time to put the whole thing out of your mind."

She doesn't believe me, thought Gail. *No one believes me.* The police report had charged her with going too fast to stop in the icy conditions. *But I had stopped at the light.* From the first, Gail had insisted that a car had bumped her from behind and had sent her vehicle spinning out into the intersection against the light, but there had been no witnesses. The car that had hit her from behind had left the scene, and the contact had not been strong enough to mark her bumper. It was only her word that it had happened that way, leaving Gail with the burden that everyone thought she had been responsible for the death of a sixteen-year-old boy, Johnnie Beeman, whose car she had struck broadside.

Gail didn't remember coming to the hospital in an ambulance, but for seemingly endless torturous days and nights, she was aware of pain like a fire-breathing beast searing her flesh. If she moved, hot coils wrapped around her. Her chest bore a great weight and all breath seemed to escape her. She floated and sank in a morass of agony. When she finally surfaced and her body slowly returned to one piece, she was told how lucky she was. With physical therapy, the doctors had assured her, she would make a complete recovery.

Angie kept a firm hand on Gail as she mounted the wide front steps of the house. The walk had been cleared of snow but a morning wind had blown white powder onto the porch steps. After the controlled warmth of the hospital, the crisp March air was like a brisk slap upon their cheeks.

"You need to get off your feet and take it easy," said Angie. "Some of the students are planning a little welcome-home party later this afternoon. I tried to get them to hold off but..." She shrugged her plump shoulders. "Anyway, try not to notice when they start banging around. Someone's bringing your favorite strawberry cheesecake."

"Somebody? Somebody like Angie Difalco?" Gail teased.

Angie laughed. "It's good to have you back." She gave Gail an impulsive hug. The Italian woman only came up to Gail's shoulders, but she had a sturdy, muscular figure that made her seem taller.

"Thanks for keeping things going, Angie. I really thought we'd have to shut the place down temporarily."

"We couldn't do that. We've worked too hard getting started."

The "we" warmed Gail's heart. From the beginning, Angie had felt a part of the business, and she'd been a lifesaver while Gail was in the hospital. Angie had hired a substitute teacher, Edith Crum, to handle reading instruction, while Angie continued to supervise the computers and, of course, take care of the paperwork in her usual efficient fashion.

"Welcome home," Angie said as she unlocked the front door. A small foyer was divided from the main hall by a second pair of etched-glass doors, which prevented drafts. A wide hall ran from the front to the back of the house and a lovely staircase curved against one wall and led to the upper floor. Gail had left her grandmother's small table flanked by two chairs in the same place they had been for years. Even the silver tray for visiting cards remained in its proper place.

The familiar smell of the old house greeted Gail warmly, a welcome-home gift after weeks in an antiseptic hospital. As the two women walked down the hall to the kitchen, Gail's cane made a thumping noise on the polished oak floors. She glanced into the original parlor, which was now transformed into a learning center with study stalls and Apple computers. The library beyond had become a small classroom for tutoring.

Everything seemed in order, and Gail drew in a deep breath of relief. The nightmare was over. She was safely home again. They had warned her about climbing stairs too soon and doing anything that might cause her to fall. She promised to be careful. After a few weeks of physical therapy, she would be able to manage the stairs and move back into her own room.

As if reading her thoughts, Angie said, "I brought down some of your things from your bedroom and will fetch more when you decide what else you might need."

A short, dead-end hall off the kitchen led to a modest maid's room and minuscule bathroom that had not been used for years. The walls were dingy with old paint and in need of Spackle to cover up myriad holes and cracks. The bathroom fixtures were gray and chipped and water pipes groaned and gurgled like someone's disgruntled stomach. The bedroom was long and narrow and a single window was bare except for a pull-down window shade. The room showed evidence of recent cleaning, fresh linens lay on the narrow bed and a bouquet of flowers sat on a scarred dresser. A large Victorian wardrobe at one end of the room had been filled with some of Gail's clothes.

"I'm sorry there wasn't time to do more," apologized Angie, watching Gail survey the room with a bleak expression.

"Everything's fine." Gail forced a bright tone. "I won't have to stay here long. Just until I can climb the stairs with ease. You're truly an angel to match your name, my Angelina."

Angie's round face flushed prettily as she gave a dismissing wave of her hand. "Just doing my job."

"Your job doesn't include maid duties."

"Don't be silly. I called the cleaning service. They're sending a woman for day work until you're stronger. Mrs. Rosales will stay each day until after you've eaten your evening meal." Angie searched Gail's face. "I was wondering if you'd like me to stay a night or two until you get settled in?"

Gail gave a forced laugh. "Heavens, no. I'm glad to be on my own." Even though the strangeness of being in this part of the house had somewhat lessened the joy of her homecoming, she certainly didn't need baby-sitting. There would be plenty of people around during the day. "You have your own family to look after. I really appreciate your husband letting you work all those extra hours here while he looked after little Jimmy."

"Does Tony good to learn what a three-year-old monster we're harboring under our roof." Angie's pretty dark eyes twinkled. "Now he knows why I have gray hairs sprouting all over my head. Nothing like an energetic Conan the Barbarian to put them there. Well, I guess I'd better run so I can get back this afternoon when the others start coming. I'd feel better if there were a telephone in here,'' said Angie.

"Oh, I can make it to the kitchen phone. No problem,'' Gail assured her. "They had me walking all over the hospital. I must have chalked up ten miles a day this last week.''

"I've put on the telephone answering machine in the library, but I don't suppose you can hear it back here. Probably just as well. I'll take care of all the messages and you can just rest. It's just two o'clock. You should be able to get a couple of hours' rest before the festivities begin.''

"What about after-school lessons?''

Angie sighed. "I don't want to go into it now...but we've had a lot of students dropping out. I guess I should have looked around more before I hired Edith Crum, but I needed somebody fast. And she came highly recommended.'' Angie frowned and then gave a dismissive shrug. "Well, she's not *you.* ''

"It's all right. I know you did the best you could. Kids don't like substitutes. Don't worry. Everything will get back to normal when I get my strength back,'' Gail assured her.

"And that means rest. Here's your medicine.'' Angie set a bottle on a small nightstand. "Stretch out and have yourself a nap.''

"Yes, I will. Now scoot along. I'll see you later this afternoon.''

Angie hesitated and then gave a merry wave of her hand. "I'll be back before the kids get out of school and start arriving for the party.'' Her solid footsteps echoed down the hall, and the front door closed with a vibrating bang.

Gail sat down on the edge of the narrow bed. She could see into the small bathroom across the hall. Angie had laid out fresh towels and brought down some toiletries from the upstairs bath but despite these personal details, the surroundings were as dreary as an ugly motel. Gail's chest tightened in a wave of uneasiness. Throughout all the pain and physical trauma that she had suffered the past few weeks, she had held on to the goal of coming home and resuming her life. But sitting there in the gloomy room, she fought a rising wave of apprehension. It must be a delayed reaction, this nebulous panic, she reasoned. The hospital nightmare was behind her and she was on her way back to the active, healthy person she had been before. Soon, she would be able to resume a full work schedule. But despite all of these positive mental reassurances, Gail couldn't shake off a sense of frightening vulnerability.

Never in her life had she felt so completely off balance. Some sixth sense was vibrating with a warning that she didn't understand.

"I'm just tired." She took a pain pill from a bottle she'd brought from the hospital. Then she stretched out on the bed and placed her cane within easy reach. She removed the pillow from under her head so she was lying flat on her back. Closing her eyes, a weariness that was as much mental as physical overtook her. She drifted off into a quiet slumber.

She must have been asleep about an hour when suddenly she was engulfed in the middle of a nightmare. Something pressed down against her face. She couldn't breathe. She tried to cry out, but her mouth was buried in the softness of a pillow. Jerking her head to one side, she thrashed her arms wildly. In her struggle one hand touched her cane leaning against the bed. With a muffled cry, she began thrashing the air wildly. The pressure on her mouth and nose eased. Dizzy, her vision narrowed, she couldn't get her breath. After a moment she flung off the pillow resting upon her face.

Winter light came through the high window and splashed dimly across the narrow room. Her breath came in gasps as her startled gaze swept the dingy walls and cracked ceiling. Pain stabbed her back as she sat up, ready to swing the cane still clutched in her sweaty hand. She looked around in bewilderment.

Everything was exactly as it had been before. Only her labored breathing broke the silence of the room. Across the hall, the bathroom door still stood open and the shower curtain was pulled back from the tiny stall the way it had been before.

Everything the same—and yet . . . She looked down at the pillow that lay innocently beside her on the bed. Hot sweat beaded on her forehead as she tried to understand what had happened. She'd never experienced such a realistic nightmare. In the midst of sleep she must have been clutching the pillow in such a way as to bury her face in it.

She took several deep breaths, trying to dispel the lingering effects of the bizarre nightmare. She reached over and picked up her medicine bottle and read the label. She frowned. The pills were the same mild painkiller she'd been taking at the hospital. Nothing to cause such a terrifying and suffocating illusion. Thoughtfully, she set the bottle back on the bedside table. The nightmare must have been triggered by the nebulous apprehension she had felt before falling asleep. The experience had been so real that her heart still thumped loudly in her chest. She felt strangely disoriented and fought a sensation of being trapped in the strange room.

She swung her feet off the bed and stood up. *I'd better get myself in hand before my mind delivers any more torments,* she told herself. At that moment, the ring of the front doorbell broke the silence of the house.

Chapter Two

Using her cane, Gail made her way slowly down the main hall toward the front of the house. A strange man stood silhouetted darkly against the inner glass doors. His features were in shadow and he wore a dark suit that contrasted with a silver glint in his black hair. How did he get in? Hadn't Angie locked the front door when she left?

"Yes?" Her voice sounded raspy. She cleared her throat and demanded in a firmer tone, "What do you want?"

As he stepped forward, a youthful face and a deep tan seemed at odds with the gray at his temples. She eyed the briefcase in his hand. A salesman of some sort?

"I'm sorry if I startled you," he began.

She frowned. "How did you get in?"

"The door was ajar."

Disbelief must have shown in her face for he quickly apologized. "I'm sorry. I assumed it was usually left open for students to come and go...so I ventured in."

His reasonable tone mocked the nervous fluttering his unexpected presence in the house had caused.

"Yes, of course. Usually that is the situation, but I've just returned home after a lengthy stay in the hospital and..."

"Yes, I know. That's why I'm here. Couldn't we sit down somewhere, Miss Richards? You look unsteady."

She frowned. "If you're selling something, please don't waste my time or yours."

He smiled at her tartness. "I haven't been a door-to-door salesman since I tried to peddle magazine subscriptions in high school...failing miserably." He stepped forward and his blue eyes deepened as his gaze swept her face. "I'm a rehabilitation counselor for Crestview Rehab Center. I like to get acquainted with new admissions before therapy begins." He held out his hand. "Curtis O'Mallory."

His hand clasp was warm and personal. Gail felt a ping of feminine regret that she wasn't looking her best. His impeccable attire mocked the jeans and ski sweater that Angie had brought for her to wear home from the hospital. Her French braid had come loose, and Gail could feel feathery wisps curling around her face. She resisted the urge to nervously smooth the tousled blond strands. Instead she quickly apologized for her abrupt reception and invited him into a small sitting room that had become her private domain on the first floor.

She led the way into the pleasant room which she'd just finished redecorating before her accident. Her grandmother's graceful old furniture and new window hangings carried out the Victorian decor. A flocked wallpaper harmonized with the fireplace's white marble mantel, and Gail had replaced an old area rug with two light blue scatter rugs that revealed the lovely oak flooring.

She noticed her visitor's look of appreciation as it traveled around the room. His eyes lingered on a backgammon set made of white oak and ivory tablesmen sitting on a small game table by the front bay window.

"Very nice," he murmured and included her in his smile.

"Please sit down." She motioned to a comfortable chair but he waited until she had eased down on the sofa, and then, without asking, he helped put a cushion to her back and offered a footstool for her feet. Gail chafed silently at her dependence on this perfect stranger.

She hated being waited on, but since her accident she'd been forced to swallow her pride. Being dependent in any situation had never been easy for her—stiff-necked pride, some people might have called it. Accepting help from this poised, frightfully good-looking stranger was especially embarrassing for her.

"Now, then," he said as he settled himself in the embrace of a wing chair. He smiled at her as if he thoroughly enjoyed sitting in old-fashioned comfort. He seemed perfectly at ease, and Gail felt a sense of satisfaction as she watched him touch the tufted arms with obvious pleasure. It was her favorite chair, too.

"Lovely." Once more his gaze brushed hers. Then he sighed and opened his briefcase. "We received a referral from Dr. Holstead that you will be starting physical therapy at Crestview. There are ways that we can make this experience less traumatic for you, Miss Richards.'' He quickly explained that the Colorado Division of Rehabilitation worked with people who had a medical disability that might prove to be a vocational handicap until they were fully recovered or retrained. "We can provide transportation to and from the center by means of an Ambu-Cab until you are ready to drive or walk the few blocks to the center."

"I hadn't even thought about that," she admitted, wondering how many other things she had overlooked. "My car was totaled and since I won't be driving for a while I haven't replaced it."

"Don't worry about it," he said with a smile that lingered in his eyes. "I'll handle all the details and you concentrate on regaining your strength. You're very lucky to be looking forward to a complete recovery."

"Yes. I feel very fortunate and ... guilty."

"Because of the fatality?" he asked gently. At her nod, he said, "I'm sure you feel deep remorse, but the situation was beyond your control, wasn't it?"

She searched his expression to see if there was skepticism lingering there. His eyes met hers in a steady, open searching that invited an honest response. "My car wouldn't have entered the intersection if it had not been struck from behind by another vehicle."

"I see."

"The police claimed I was going too fast for the icy conditions—but I had come to a complete stop when the car behind me sent my Volvo spinning into the intersection. The teenager's car was racing to beat the yellow light and ... and there wasn't anything I could do."

"Was the back of your car damaged?"

"No, the contact wasn't hard enough to even mark my bumper, so the police don't believe me. I told them that the shove was just enough to send my car sliding forward on the ice."

"Doesn't take much to make a sled out of a car ... especially on a hill," he agreed. "It's a scary feeling, all right. Sometimes a half-dozen cars are involved in chain accidents on icy roads. And the car that bumped you?"

"Left the scene."

He frowned. "So the driver of the car who bumped yours either panicked or fled the scene to avoid involvement?"

"Unfortunately, there were no witnesses."

"And you were alone?" There was a slight questioning lilt to his tone.

She rather resented his skeptical tone, as if he found it hard to believe she went places by herself. "Yes, I was alone. I'd been to a party given by one of our young students, Keith Karbough. A strictly nonalcoholic affair. It was a birthday celebration and I'd promised I'd attend. So in spite of the snowstorm I made a brief appearance and then left early because of the weather." She passed a hand over her eyes. "I don't think I'll ever forget that crunch of metal and breaking glass...and...and then learning that a young boy had been killed."

"It wasn't your fault," he said quietly. "You're just as much a victim as anyone. You could have been paralyzed for life the way the front of your car must have been crushed. I know that the death of the young boy weighs heavily on you, but you can't carry around a load of guilt. Under the circumstances, there was nothing you could have done to avoid the accident."

She lifted her head and smiled at him gratefully. "You believe me?"

"Of course." His dark blue eyes were soft and steady as they met hers. "I read the account published in the newspaper...which varies from yours, of course, but I trust my intuition when it comes to people." His smile was reassuring. "I believe the accident happened just as you said. I don't think you're a woman who is afraid to face up to responsibility, Miss Richards."

The need for his approval took her by surprise. "Gail...please," she offered. "And thank you."

He closed up his briefcase and then leaned back in the chair as if drinking in the delight of his surroundings. For a long moment they sat in companionable silence.

A late afternoon sun shone through the front lace curtains and spread a dappled pattern upon the polished oak flooring. Two authentic Tiffany lamp shades caught the light in a rainbow of color. A melodious ticking of a black and gold ormolu clock sitting on the mantel was harmonious with the quiet, reassuring mood that his presence had brought to her.

Gail watched his face, searching to know him better on some nonverbal level. His expression was gentle, relaxed, and yet there was an alertness in his well-conditioned body that exuded energy and intelligence. His left hand lay casually on the arm of the chair, and she chided herself for feeling an inner satisfaction when a quick glance determined that he wasn't wearing a wedding band. It had been a long time since she'd been interested in a man's marital status.

"Your home is very gracious and warm." His gaze settled on her honey blond hair and greenish-gray eyes. "A reflection of quiet beauty—much like yourself."

The compliment brought an unexpected warmth to her cheeks. Even though an inner voice warned her that this man was a professional counselor and his job was to deftly handle people, she couldn't deny the quiver of pleasure his attention gave her.

"I inherited the property from my aunt." She told him about her decision to keep it by turning some of the rooms into a learning center.

"Sounds as if you made the right decision. I'm glad that rehab will be able to help you out... lessen some of the problems of getting back into full swing. You've come through a traumatic experience. It can't have been easy."

Inviting an honesty that made her want to reach out to him, she almost shared the apprehension that kept cold fear within her. Would he think her unstable if she confessed to the nebulous apprehension eating away at her? What if she told him about the horrible nightmare that had made her clutch a pillow so tightly that she couldn't breathe? As these tortured thoughts raced through her mind, he leaned forward.

"What is it, Gail? You've suddenly gone rigid. And your eyes have changed color. A moment ago they were feathered softly with green. Now they're almost flat gray, as if bleached by some deep emotion."

Gail moistened her dry lips. If she were honest with him, what then? Would he insist on a psychiatric evaluation? She certainly was above such foolishness as to interpret Curtis O'Mallory's interest as anything but professional. His ease in the situation betrayed his expertise in handling rehab clients like herself. That was his job. He was here to gain her confidence and set her at ease for the rehabilitation program ahead of her. If she revealed her inner anxieties, he might change his mind and decide that she wasn't ready to begin an intense physical therapy program until she had some psychological evaluations.

"I'm a good listener," he prodded.

Even if she had wanted to be honest with him, Gail doubted if she could verbalize the deep dread that seemed unfounded. When she had tried to explain her feelings to her doctor before she left the hospital, he had given her a tired smile. "Just a reaction to the physical trauma that your body has suffered." He'd patted her hand, and she had felt foolish and juvenile. She certainly wasn't going to make a fool of herself by expressing her anxieties to this personable counselor.

She forced a smile. "There's nothing to tell. I'm concerned about getting back to normal as soon as possible, that's all."

He looked at the hands she had clenched in her lap, and then raised his gaze to her face. He waited. The penetrating scrutiny of his dark blue eyes made her feel defenseless. She might have confessed her inner turmoil if Angie hadn't stuck her head through the doorway at that moment.

"Oh, there you are." She looked startled when she saw Gail wasn't alone. "Oh, I'm sorry. I didn't know you had company."

"This is Mr. O'Mallory from Crestview Rehab Center. Mrs. Angelina Difalco, my assistant," said Gail, making the introductions.

Curtis, instantly on his feet, smiled and held out his hand. "Pleased to meet you, Mrs. Difalco."

Angie's eyes traveled over his deeply tanned face and his well-conditioned body. "Well, well. A skier, I'll bet."

"I like to think so." He grinned. "I confess I'd be a ski bum if I had the chance."

Angie gave Gail a knowing look that said, Wow!

"Mr. O'Mallory is a rehabilitation counselor," Gail said rather primly.

"Curtis, please." His soft smile in Gail's direction made the request more personal than professional.

He's good, thought Gail. She'd never been in therapy of any kind but she could see how it would be easy to get one's emotions tangled up when relating to someone who was as smooth as this counselor.

"Then you'll be looking after Gail," prodded Angie.

"I'll do my best."

"Good, and you'll stay for the welcome-home party. We're setting up refreshments now. I gave Keith

Karbough my keys, so he was here earlier bringing in a few things."

"That's why the front door was opened," Gail said, feeling foolish for being so uneasy earlier. It was just nerves that made her so jumpy. Everything was under control. Wasn't it? She started to get up, but Angie stopped her.

"Just stay where you are, Gail. We can fill our plates in the dining room and gather in here. Would you like to help, Mr. O'Mallory? Bring in some of the presents?"

"Sure."

"Presents?" Gail gasped. This was getting out of hand. She wished she'd been asked before the preparations had been made. She'd never felt less like celebrating in her life. Good intentions of friends were sometimes worse than neglect.

She fixed a smile on her face as the well-wishers came swarming in. A pair of giggling girls enrolled for special tutoring gave her some handmade get-well cards. Several faces among the secondary students were missing, and Gail realized that they'd lost a lot of pupils because of her absence. For a moment, concern over more expenses and the loss of income deepened the lines in her forehead. Then she firmly pushed the worry aside and forced herself to respond positively to all the well-wishers.

She thanked Keith Karbough and his mother for a book on the bestseller list.

"We were utterly devastated about the accident," commiserated Mrs. Karbough. "And feel so responsible. If Keith hadn't been so set on having the party, this wouldn't have happened."

"Don't be ridiculous," answered Gail in a sharper tone than she had intended. She quickly turned to the skinny junior-high boy. "You don't have anything to feel guilty about. Your party was lovely and the accident had nothing to do with you." She saw tears about to swell up in his eyes. "It's okay, Keith, really." She took his hand and squeezed it.

The boy gave her a wan smile, but his eyes were like those of a wounded pup. Gail fumed silently. Couldn't his mother see what she was doing to the boy? The only reason Gail had gone to Keith's party on such a snowy night was to reassure the youngster of her affection. His arrogant mother refused to accept the fact that her son was dyslexic. Keith was making progress with reading but not fast enough to suit his domineering mother. The boy stayed close to Gail's chair.

Gail was delighted to see her favorite adult student, Mr. Devitto. He was a fifty-year-old cab driver who was taking reading instruction on about a third-grade level. He had brought her a box of candy and boldly leaned over and kissed her cheek. "We pray for you," he said.

The old house vibrated with laughter and chatter. Gail's head began to ache from the noise, but she kept a smile on her lips. Her students had brought balloons, cakes, pies and ice cream. Once or twice, Gail caught Curtis O'Mallory's eyes on her. He smiled and winked as if to say, Hang in there.

Edith Crum, the substitute teacher whom Angie had hired, was a plump, bouncing little woman almost as broad as she was tall.

"This is Miss Crum." Angie had a nervous edge to her voice as she brought the woman over to Gail. She waited anxiously for Gail's reaction.

"Thank you for helping us out," said Gail, thinking that the pudgy woman was a good feminine match for the Pillsbury Doughboy. Her nut-brown hair was a mass of permed curls bouncing away from her round face and dimpled cheeks. A frilly blouse, which added several additional inches to her already ample bosom, and a gathered skirt did little to hide the thickness of her hips and legs.

"This is all quite strange to me," she confided with a jiggling of her double chin. "When I read about the accident in the paper, I said to myself, 'Edie, you'd better get yourself over there and see if they're needing a substitute teacher to fill in for that poor Miss Richards.'" She smiled broadly at Angie. "I think Mrs. Difalco was mighty happy to see me. She looked a bit frazzled, if you want to know the truth. But we have everything under control now, don't we?" She practically clapped her hands with joy.

Gail could tell that Angie was silently groaning. "Do you substitute in public schools, Miss Crum?" *Where did this lady come from?*

"Yes...I haven't had a regular classroom for years. I prefer hopping around to different schools. Things don't get boring that way. A day here and a day there. I've been in every school in the Denver district." She reached out and grabbed Keith, who was standing by

Gail's chair, and gave him a bear hug that made him wince. "Taught his class last December, didn't I, honey?"

Keith nodded without enthusiasm. Gail found herself wanting to put an apple in the woman's full, ever-moving lips.

"All these machines—computers." She moaned. "I'm all for progress, you understand, but I have to question whether machines can replace teachers." Her full face wrinkled with a smile, but her round eyes were quite cold. "I think a good set of readers in the hands of a competent teacher can't be beat."

Gail wanted to retort that her enrollment was made up of students who had failed because a single teaching method using standard readers had not fit their pattern of learning, but she wasn't up to a heated academic discussion. She made some vague, polite responses and silently vowed that she would dismiss Edie Crum as quickly as possible.

"Would you like another piece of cake, Miss Crum?" asked Angie, guiding her away and giving Gail an apologetic look over her shoulder.

Gail was glad when the festivities were finally over and Angie was seeing everyone out the door. Curtis lingered until the room was empty. "It's easy to see that your pupils have a great affection for you, Gail."

"Every one of them is special to me," she confessed.

"Yes, I can tell that. I have a little girl in my case load who's been in and out of Crestview because of a birth deformity. We've tried tutors from time to time because of her erratic schooling, but she really needs some extra reading instruction. I have to warn you, she's something of a brat. She's been responsible for putting red dye in the whirlpool machines, tying shoelaces in knots, and letting air out of wheelchair tires."

Gail laughed. "Sounds as if she's got energy to burn."

"Maybe we could arrange for her to enroll in your reading center... if you have any openings."

"Any additional pupil would be welcome," she said honestly. "We'd be happy to work with her." *How astute he is,* thought Gail. *Either that or he's a mind reader. He knows I'm concerned about making ends meet.*

"Good." He started to say something more, but Angie came back into the room with a package.

"Somebody left it on the porch. Probably didn't want to come to the party. Another present, I bet." She laid the box in Gail's lap.

One of her former teacher friends, thought Gail as she tore away the wrappings. A card with a Mother Goose drawing on the front lay inside. Gail opened it and read a verse printed in a bright red crayon:

"Diddle diddle dumpling, poor young John,
Killed in the street, his lifeblood gone.
One shoe off... and one shoe on,
Dead in the street, poor young John."

Gail's gaze fixed in horror on the contents of the box. A boy's worn tennis shoe lay there—covered with blood!

Chapter Three

"Heaven help us!" gasped Angie, looking down at the blood-splattered shoe. She swept the box and wrapping paper off Gail's lap, stammering, "I—I'm sorry... I had no idea."

Curtis quickly moved to Gail's side and sat down on the couch beside her. Her face was blanched and pinched, and when she looked at him, eyes wide with horror, he took her hand and covered it firmly with both of his. "Just a sick joke. Don't let it get to you."

The pain in her eyes stabbed at him. He wanted to smooth away the quiver of her lips and touch the sweet fullness of her mouth. It was all he could do not to pull her close against his chest and stroke her tenderly. He was startled by the force of his protective feelings. An emotion he couldn't identify swept through him, and he warned himself that Gail Richards might easily appeal to him on a level that went beyond professional obligation.

"Why would... someone...?" she stammered.

His jaw hardened with rage. "For kicks."

"How... could they?" she asked.

"Probably kids... maybe buddies of Johnnie Beeman's... using this stupid way to vent their grief."

Angie's black eyes snapped. "Well, I'd like to get my hands on the culprits. I'd knock some sense into their heads. Gail has enough to bear without putting up with such nonsense. I think we ought to report this to the police."

"No." Gail shook her head firmly. Taking a deep breath, she straightened up. "No harm's done. Let it go."

Curtis nodded. "I think that's the best thing to do. This kind of joke peters out when no one pays any attention." Reluctantly he let go of her hand. Feeling her soft flesh clinging to his had been a sensuous pleasure, and the contact had stirred him more than he was ready to admit. The impulse to stroke her cheek and touch her hair startled him. He drew back, forcing his thoughts into channels of detached perspective.

Angie dumped the box and its vile contents into a trash basket with the rest of the party wrappings. Gail bit her lower lip and closed her eyes for a moment as if to shut out the whole scene.

Curtis watched the color drain from her face. "We have a fine psychologist on the staff," he said. "Would you like me to make an appointment..."

Her eyes flew open. "No. *I'm all right!*" She emphasized each word. "For heaven's sake, don't try to make me into some kind of a mental case."

"I'm not trying to make you into anything," he said quietly. The pulse in her throat was beating wildly. "Anyone would be shaken up," he assured her. "You might find it helpful to share your feelings with a professional."

"I'm perfectly capable of handling this malicious mischief, Mr. O'Mallory." Her chin jutted out slightly as if daring him to deny that capability.

He loved the way her eyes were suddenly flashing. He held out his hands in a gesture or surrender. "It was only a suggestion."

"I can handle my own affairs," she responded stiffly.

"Yes, I believe you can. You appear to be a very self-directed independent woman."

"Too damn independent, if you ask me," said Angie with affectionate concern. "Wouldn't hurt Gail none to accept a little help now and again."

"Please, don't fuss," she pleaded.

"Well, I think you've had enough company for one day," said Curtis, standing up. He knew that she wasn't going to accept any expression of protection from him. "I'll take my leave and look forward to seeing you at the center tomorrow afternoon. Shall I arrange for the Ambu-Cab to pick you up about two o'clock?"

She nodded. "And...thank you." Her eyes deepened into a startling shade of aquamarine as she looked up at him. "I really appreciate your being here."

He felt a peculiar tightening in his chest and something akin to an electric spark jolted him. *Steady, fellow,* he schooled himself. *Professional distance, remember?* He forced a briskness into his tone. "Just doing my job. You'll like Crestview. I promise that we'll have you running the four-forty in no time.''

"That would be a miracle, indeed." There was a teasing lilt to her voice that he hadn't heard before. "I couldn't run that before the accident." A weak smile hovered at the corners of her mouth.

She had lips made for smiling—or kissing, he thought before he managed to bring his thoughts back to business. "You'll hate us for working you so hard... but if you don't quit..."

"I'm not a quitter."

He smiled down at her. "No, I don't think you are." He suspected that her dogged determination accounted for the astounding recovery she'd made in such a short time. She'd been up and about as soon as possible after the operation on her back. After he had read Gail Richards's record, he'd admired her valiant spirit and had been ready to like his new client, but he hadn't been prepared for the impact she'd made on his personal feelings. The private time they shared earlier had brought deep, unexpected pleasure. "I'll see you at the center tomorrow."

Gail held out her hand to him. "Thanks again."

His fingers closed over hers and lingered in a gentle squeeze. "Till tomorrow, then."

After he'd gone, Angie chuckled. "Why do I get the feeling that Mr. O'Mallory is going to enjoy looking after you."

"Don't be silly," chided Gail. She knew better than to think that the attractive rehab counselor had more than a routine interest in her. She had never felt less attractive in her whole life.

CURTIS DROVE to Crestview Rehabilitation Center about five blocks away. The two-story brick building stood back from the street and was partially hidden by drifts of evergreens and tall barren oak trees. At the moment everything was covered with winter snow, which softened the noise from nearby busy streets and lent a hushed tranquillity to the scene. Curtis followed a circular driveway around to the side of the building and pulled into the parking spot bearing his name. He turned off the engine and sat there with his forehead creased in thought.

He had been more disturbed by the bloody shoe incident than he had admitted. The unexpected viciousness had appalled him. He just hoped that this was an ugliness that would *not* be repeated. He was worried that the perpetrator might not be satisfied with one malicious offering and might keep it up. Gail was obviously shaken by her part in the fatality and had suffered greatly over the young man's death. The police had not been easy on her, charging her with careless driving, and dismissing her story of another car bumping hers from behind. Without any witnesses, it was only her word, and there wasn't anything she could do to clear herself.

He remembered the soft, appealing touch of her hand in his and the way her eyes deepened into that rare shade of blue-green when she smiled. The muscles in his jaw stiffened when he remembered the way her face had paled when she opened the repugnant package.

Without the slightest reservation he was ready to act as a barrier between her and this kind of despicable harassment. *Part of my job as a counselor,* he told himself. His reaction would be the same for anyone under similar circumstances, wouldn't it?

He'd always been ready to go that extra mile for any of his clients. His supervisor had lectured him more than once about giving so much of himself to his cases. He couldn't help it. Every handicapped child, stricken teenager or shattered adult mattered to him, and that was one of the reasons he had remained single. The demands of his job left little time or energies for a personal life. Until today he'd never been tempted to relate to a client in a personal way.

He would be lying to himself if he denied that he found Gail Richards extremely appealing and attractive. She was the kind of woman who could stir a man's desire with a soft smile and a teasing glint in her eyes. He loved the way she related to her students, and he was impressed by the way they fell over themselves to please her. Why would anyone want to cause her a moment's pain?

He sighed, got out of the car and went inside the building. His office was a corner room at the far end of the main hall. Myra Monet, his attractive and efficient secretary, was putting some papers on his desk when he came in.

"Some letters to sign," she said in her brisk tone. She was a pretty woman, a divorcée in her early thirties. Good complexion with slightly tinted chestnut hair falling to her shoulders. She took good care of her lithe, athletic body. She was always the first one to sign up for a charity race, and last summer, she'd talked Curtis into joining her for some early morning jogging. Curtis suspected she used exercise to release a lot of pent-up emotional tension. She managed the office and him with energetic dispatch.

"I finished up the monthly reports and completed the computer printout," she told him, satisfaction sparkling in her brown eyes.

"You're the best, Myra," Curtis said as he opened his briefcase and handed her the papers that Gail had signed. "Forms for the new client, Gail Richards. She's set up to start therapy tomorrow afternoon. I'll confirm it with the P.T. department. We need to arrange for an Ambu-Cab pickup at two o'clock."

Myra nodded, glancing over the form. "The Learning House? I've driven by there... an old Victorian mansion, isn't it?"

Curtis nodded. "Miss Richards has converted the ground floor into a reading center. Seems to be doing quite well. I crashed a welcome-home party for her." He remembered how it had ended and the muscles in his face hardened.

"It must have turned out to be a drag," she said, eyeing his grim expression. "What's this gal like?"

"Very..." Curtis searched for the right word and gave up. "Nice." He avoided Myra's eyes as he sat down at his desk. *Beautiful. Appealing. Sensitive. Disturbing.*

"Nice?" Myra echoed. Her mouth tightened. "Isn't she the one who ran into some teenager while DUI? Coming home from a party, wasn't she?"

"The accident wasn't her fault," answered Curtis firmly. "And she tested clean... no alcohol in her system. The truth of the matter is that Gail had her car under control when she was shoved into the intersection. The driver responsible for the fatality left the scene.''

Myra pursed her mouth. "That's *her* story."

"I don't think Gail's lying," Curtis said curtly. "She's a very sincere, sensitive woman. Gail's taking a lot of flak for something that wasn't her fault."

Curtis's use of the client's first name didn't get past his secretary. Nor his readiness to defend the woman. Myra's feminine radar began to flicker.

"Any calls?" asked Curtis, feeling uncomfortable under her speculative gaze.

She brought Curtis up to date on some telephone messages. She paused on her way out the door and asked him if he'd like to join a small group that was taking the ski train to Vail over the weekend.

He declined.

"Maybe next time." Her brown eyes searched his face.

"Maybe."

She shrugged and left his office.

Curtis felt a little guilty about treating her so briskly. The truth was that Myra's aggressive manner had destroyed the chances of anything but a casual friendship developing between them. The few times they'd been in each other's company outside the office, he'd kept his guard up.

There was an intensity about Myra that was a little disconcerting. He couldn't quite put his finger on it. She was a hard worker, always going beyond the requirements of her job description. Sometimes he grew a little weary of thanking her for all the extra things she did, and he always felt uneasy that he wasn't giving her credit for everything he should.

Myra never talked about her ex-husband, but Curtis had the feeling that she was still emotionally shattered by the breakup of her marriage. Apparently there had been a child, but for some reason the father had gained custody of the little boy.

In any case, he'd decided not to pursue any off-job relationship with his secretary...or anyone else who worked at Crestview, even though some of the nurses were quite open about their readiness to accept any date he might offer. He smiled, thinking about pretty Ellyn McPherson, a floor nurse who had dogged his footsteps when she first started working at Crestview. Her crush on him had been obvious to everyone and he'd taken a lot of ribbing about it. He found himself checking the cafeteria before he'd go in for a cup of coffee, and he'd leave ten minutes earlier to avoid having her ask for a ride to the bus stop. After a while, the pretty brunette's attentions wandered in a different direction and Curtis breathed a relieved "Hooray." He never got involved with his clients, either.

With businesslike efficiency, Curtis reached over and marked his calendar for the next day. "Gail—two o'clock." Then he surprised himself by underlining it three times.

WHEN GAIL ARRIVED the next afternoon, she was met by a young man with sun-bleached blond hair and a ready smile.

"Ready for your limousine ride?" asked the grinning orderly, as he helped her from the Ambu-Cab.

"I don't need a wheelchair," she protested as he eased her down into one.

"No problem. This is the P.T. Special. Guaranteed to deliver you to your destination with a smile." He gave her a mock bow. "Larry Smith, your personal chauffeur."

His grin was infectious and did wonders to settle the quiver of nervousness in her stomach. She'd been worried about how difficult the physical therapy was going to be. Maybe she wouldn't be able to do all the prescribed exercises. She had a fourteen-inch scar down the middle of her back. The muscles that the surgeon had cut in order to implant two eight-inch stainless steel rods sent a hot burning sensation around her waist at the slightest movement. Gail had seen the X-rays of her lower back, which showed the quarter-inch-thick rods and intricate steel clamps gripping her spinal cord like claws. Her doctor had assured her that proper exercise was the way back to normal mobility. But he had cautioned her against climbing stairs until her balance was back to normal because of the danger of falling. Gail intended to heed his advice. At times she felt as if she might break apart in the middle like a mended sawdust doll.

"And away we go!" said Larry, a shock of blond hair falling over one eye as he deftly maneuvered the wheelchair into the building. "We will take the scenic route. The P.T. rooms are in the new addition."

He kept up a running monologue as spinning wheels hummed along the polished floor. Mimicking a tour guide's voice, he announced, "As we pass our award-losing cafeteria, inhale the dubious odors of yesterday's dinner, which is today's lunch and tomorrow's mysterious potluck. Our cook believes in recycling.''

Gail chuckled. She appreciated Larry's attempt to lighten the situation. Everyone they met had a greeting or smile for the attendant, and more than one young nurse blushed deeply as he grinned at her.

The therapy rooms were in a separate wing of the building and resembled a well-equipped gym, complete with water therapy facilities and swimming pool. Larry delivered Gail to a young woman whose name tag identified her as Beth Scott, Aide.

''Here's Miss Richards, Beth,'' said Larry. ''Treat her nice, hear?''

''Don't you worry none. We'll give her a right good time,'' she promised, giving Larry the same smile he'd merited from everyone else. Gail knew from her accent that the aide was probably from Oklahoma or Texas.

''Good enough,'' Larry said with a grin. ''When you're finished, Miss Richards, they'll call me and I'll take you to the Ambu-Cab.'' He gave Beth an engaging wink and disappeared down the hall.

Stocky, round-faced, somewhere in her early twenties, Beth had pretty brown eyes that harmonized with her sandy hair. Her steady gaze held a glint of envy as she appraised Gail's fair complexion and blond French braid.

With smooth efficiency, she pushed Gail into a room equipped for water therapy, helped Gail undress and put on a one-piece bathing suit. Then she instructed Gail to lie down on a canvas stretcher that was extended over a large tank of water.

Gently Beth lowered the stretcher until Gail was slightly immersed. Under Beth's guidance, Gail began to move her arms and legs in the water. They were suddenly extremely light and Gail felt herself relaxing.

"Nice," she murmured.

"Most patients like it," Beth said and chatted easily about the benefits of water therapy. She told Gail that she'd worked two years at Crestview and was lonesome for her family in Denton, Texas. "Sure wish summer would get here so I could go see them again. I hate Colorado winters, don't you?" Then she put a hand over her mouth. "Oh, I'm sorry. You probably don't want to be reminded of your car accident. Sometimes I just rattle off at the mouth without thinking."

"It's all right," Gail assured her, but she hated the idea that everyone in this place probably knew she'd been involved in a fatal accident.

After ten minutes in the water, Beth helped her dress again and wheeled her into the next room.

"One of the therapists will be with you in a minute," Beth assured her. She left Gail lying on an exercise table inside a small curtained cubicle.

Relaxed from her water therapy, Gail closed her eyes. She felt strangely at peace with herself. Everything was going to be all right. Last night she'd tested her courage to stay by herself in the house. It hadn't been easy. She had lain in her bed, listening to the groaning bathroom pipes and the rustle of tree branches outside the window, watching as dark shadows stretched across the room. Her recent suffocating nightmare rested uneasily on her, and it had been after midnight before she'd finally fallen into an exhausted sleep.

A rustle beside her high exercising table brought her back to the present. She opened her eyes. Two large brown-black eyes stared back at her. At first, Gail thought she was looking into the round face of a dwarf, then she realized it was a child who was staring at her. Wild curly hair like a red muff framed a freckled face and made the little girl's head appear too large for her skinny childish body. Large dark eyes were unblinking as they fixed on Gail's. The homely little girl was leaning on a pair of crutches.

"Hi," said Gail, trying not to show her surprise.

"What's wrong with you?" she demanded with childish bluntness.

Taken aback for a moment, Gail stammered. "I—I was in a car wreck."

"We got lots of those." The little girl sniffed as if she were hoping for something a little more interesting. "A lot worse than you," she added as if to cut Gail down to proper size.

Gail couldn't help smiling. The girl's frankness was refreshing. She much preferred children who displayed a strong sense of themselves. "What about you?" she asked, deciding to follow the child's frank approach.

"Birth defect." She shrugged her thin shoulders. "They're shifting some of my muscles around so I can walk better. I was born in Wyoming. Ever been there?"

"A few times. What's your name?"

"Scuffy."

"That's your real name?"

"Nope. My pa said I looked like a stray cat from the moment I was born . . . so nobody calls me by my real name." She wrinkled up her nose. "Marjorie Jane Snodgrass. Ugh."

"That's a nice name."

Scuffy gave her a disgusted what-do-you-know look and demanded, "What's your name?"

"Gail."

"That's it? Just Gail?"

"Gail Richards."

She cocked her tousled red head and thought for a moment. "Are you?"

"What?"

"Rich?"

Gail smothered a grin. "Afraid not."

Scuffy sighed. "I thought so. I guess you won't be handing out candy or anything?" she said hopefully. "You're not bad looking. Maybe Larry will take a liking to you."

"You think so?" Gail was amused by her solemnity.

"Yeah. He likes all kinds of girls. Course you may be a little old for him. I heard him say he likes them young and willing. You know what I mean?"

Gail was afraid she did. "How old are you, Scuffy?"

"Eight. But I'm old for my age," she confided in a solemn tone. "They say I've grown up fast . . . in and out of hospitals so much." Her dark eyes glinted. "I keep my ears open. Learn a lot of stuff.'' Scuffy eyed Gail frankly. ''Are you a blabbermouth?''

''I don't think so.''

The child studied her and then shrugged as if she'd measured Gail and found her wanting. ''I got to get back to my room before Hatchet-Face Tewsberry has a hissy fit. That's the head nurse up on my floor. She doesn't like me talking to other patients.''

''Why not?''

''She says I make up stories—but I don't. Just 'cause my legs look like pretzels doesn't mean my brains are made out of spaghetti, does it?''

''Of course not. You seem like a very bright little girl.'' Gail smiled. ''And I'm glad to know you.''

Scuffy gave Gail one of her unblinking stares. Then she disappeared through the curtains like a monkey swinging along on two sticks.

She must be the little girl Curtis had mentioned, thought Gail. He'd said she was an institutional brat...and Scuffy seemed to fit the description. Gail chuckled. It would be a challenge to work with her. For the first time in weeks, she began to see beyond her recovery to the joys of teaching again.

The white curtain walls were suddenly swept away and a tall, lanky woman, with boyishly cut brown hair introduced herself. ''I'm Roberta Benson. I'll be your therapist, Miss Richards.''

Gail felt a spurt of uneasiness. The therapist reminded Gail of a hard-driving gym teacher she'd had in high school. Her expression did not invite confidences. She wore a white tunic and slacks and there was a no-nonsense air about her that matched her next words. "It's my job to work you harder than a mule driver. When you think you can't do one more exercise, I'll see that you do."

She began to outline a program of table exercises, muscle-building activities and supervised walking on treadmills. "How fast you regain your health is really up to you."

She waited for Gail to respond.

"I understand." Did the woman come on this way to all her patients? *Or is it just me?* thought Gail.

"Good." Roberta's angular face was devoid of makeup and pretty long eyelashes seemed misplaced over bleached hazel eyes. Her body was well toned. Muscular arms and hard thighs stretched the cloth of her white medical outfit, and Gail thought she had the largest hands for a woman that she'd ever seen. She couldn't suppress a quiver of apprehension when the woman took a firm hold on one of Gail's legs.

"Let's begin. Tighten the muscles. Good. Now lift this leg as I do the work for you."

The exercises were demanding and Gail concentrated on following instructions the therapist gave in crisp, efficient tones. Roberta's noncommittal expression never changed. Gail couldn't tell if she'd done well for her first time or not.

After the table exercises, Roberta took Gail into a gymlike room and set her to working with weights and walking along parallel bars. Only stubborn pride kept Gail working as hard as she could until Roberta said, "All right, that's enough for today."

Beth brought in the wheelchair. "Larry will be here in a few minutes. How'd the first day go?"

"Fine," said Gail, but Beth smiled as if she knew every muscle in Gail's body was painful.

When Curtis O'Mallory walked in the door, an unreasonable spurt of joy shot through Gail.

"Hi. You survived?" he asked, giving her that caring smile of his.

"Just barely, I'm afraid." Then she brightened. "I'm tired, but it's a good kind of tired."

"Good. I was wondering if—" he hesitated "—if I could stop back this evening and get that package you received yesterday."

A chill went through Gail as if someone had just opened a door to a bitter wind. All the ugliness swept back. That unnamed apprehension began to quiver in her stomach. "Why?"

"I told a good friend of mine who's a detective about it...and Lieutenant Lamont said it wouldn't hurt for him to take a look at it."

"How could you call in the police without consulting with me first?" There was fire in her eyes, and her chin jutted out angrily.

He made a quick apology, trying to explain his concern. "I'm sorry...but I really decided it was best—"

"*You* decided."

Her tone whittled him down with the truth. *I should have consulted her.* He'd let his concern discount her reaction to his interference. She was one independent woman. He held out his hands in a surrendering gesture. "You're right, of course. I shouldn't have called the lieutenant without your approval."

"I thought we agreed not to make a big deal out of it. Someone made a bad joke, that's all."

"If that's all it is, no harm done. If not— Well, it would be better to find out what we can before it goes any further, don't you agree?"

He didn't want to worry her, but his friend Lieutenant Lamont had not dismissed the bloody shoe and nursery rhyme as a practical joke. In fact, the detective had listened in ominous silence as Curtis explained the situation. Then Lamont had sworn, "Blast it all. Not another one."

Chapter Four

The woman unlocked the door of the small frame house and stamped her boots free of snow as she tossed her purse on the hall end table. She sorted through the mail she'd taken from the porch mailbox. Nothing but advertisements. Her birthday had been last week, but nobody had remembered.

Her house sat in an undeveloped area just outside the city limits. She liked the privacy and the rent was reasonable. Her footsteps echoed in the shadowy hall as she climbed the stairs to her bedroom at the front of the house. Another demanding day. Muscles at the back of her head knotted with mounting pain. Keeping her emotions under tight control was like harnessing a wild energy that threatened to blow her apart.

She shed her work clothes, put the soiled ones in the hamper and pulled on a pair of jeans and a man's shirt. She shuffled in soft bedroom slippers downstairs to her small kitchen and took a can of beer out of the fridge. She was just popping the lid when she heard something at the back door.

She stiffened and then relaxed when she identified a pitiful mewing. She opened the door. A shivering young gray cat was hunched on the doorstep, his fur coated with icicles, and his whiskers dropping with snow.

"You poor thing." She stooped over and picked the cat up, murmuring reassurances as she brought it into the kitchen. Her beer forgotten, she quickly ran some warm water in the sink. An expansive feeling of righteousness filled her. She began to recite contentedly. "Pussycat, pussycat, where have you been? I've been to London to see the Queen. Pussycat, pussycat what did you there? I frightened a little mouse under her chair."

She laughed as she stroked the cat with a warm wash rag. "There now, that's better, isn't it?" she said in a falsetto voice. "Much better. Now for a nice bath. Here we go..."

She lowered the cat into the warm basin of water but the animal struck out in protest. His paws ejected curved claws. One of them swiped her arm as he tried to scramble out of the sink. Her beaming expression changed to one of ugliness as blood from the scratch on her arm dripped into the water.

Her grasp was no longer loving as she forced the cat under the water, holding it there until it ceased to struggle. When it became placid in her hands she said, "There now, that's better." Happily she resumed her bathing of the cat, holding up the limp head and letting water fall over its body. "Now then, we'll dry you off nice."

She folded a towel around its body and sat down in a chair. She rubbed the gray fur, drying it as she murmured contentedly, "I love little pussy, her coat is so

warm...and if I don't hurt her she'll do me no
harm...so I'll not pull her tail, nor drive her
away...but pussy and I very gently will play."

She hummed contentedly as she brushed the soft fur
for a long time in slow, languid strokes. Then she
laughed and held the cat out in front of her. The mirth
in her throat died away as her eyes fell on the ugly
scratch on her arm. Her eyes lost their soft glaze. Why
did everything end up hurting her? She tried her best.
Gave of herself and made sacrifices. And nobody appreciated it. Not even a stray cat.

She walked over to the kitchen door, opened it and
threw the dead animal out into the snow. Bitterness
and a sense of utter desolation slithered through her.
Her mouth was held in a tight angry line as she picked
up her can of beer and went into the living room. She
flipped on the television set, eased down on the couch
and sipped her drink as she watched the evening news.

She looked at the screen for several unseeing moments. She tenderly touched a bruised spot on her
shoulder where the cane had hit. Then she got up, put
on her coat and went out of the house again.

Chapter Five

Curtis drove to Gail's house after dinner. He entertained a moment of uneasiness when he found every window of the Victorian mansion dark. A jagged roofline loomed darkly against the night sky and banks of snow gave an eerie aspect to the exterior of the house. Curtis parked in a driveway that ran along one side of the house to a stable that had been converted into a double garage. He mounted steps at the side of an old-fashioned veranda, which hugged the front of the house. A streetlight sent his shadow playing across the panels of the double front door as he pressed the doorbell.

Muffled chimes echoed inside the house. Then silence. A dog barked in a distant yard but the night held an unearthly stillness that caused a warm sweat to bead on his neck. He rang the doorbell a second time and then knocked loudly. Impatient, he turned the brass doorknob. The front door was locked this time.

"Gail! Gail," he called loudly.

No answer.

He was about to go around to the back door when he glimpsed a movement inside as the inner glass doors opened.

"Who is it?" Her voice cracked.

"Curt—Curtis O'Mallory." He cupped his eyes and peered in and at that moment a foyer light came on and blinded him for a moment.

He saw Gail as she fumbled with the lock and then stepped back, getting her cane out of the way of the door opening. She wore an aqua lounging suit in a plush fabric that hugged her lithe frame and enhanced the color of her eyes. Lines of fatigue and lavender shadows on her cheeks were deepened by a look of anxiety that made Curtis want to reach out and soothe her.

"Are you all right?" he asked anxiously.

She nodded.

"When I saw the place dark..." He began.

"I'm sorry. I—I forgot you were coming." She turned and led the way into the hall, stopping to touch a switch that sent a high chandelier into a blaze of light.

Curtis followed her into the small sitting room where they had talked before. He waited until she had turned on a small lamp and sat down on the couch before he let anxiety spew out as anger. "Why isn't someone here with you?"

Color flared into her cheeks. "Because I choose to be alone. I'm used to looking after myself."

He'd seen belligerent pride in all its forms. Usually he welcomed it, but looking at Gail's slightly quivering chin, he sensed that some of her independence was a cover-up for a deep-seated fear. "Very admirable, but in this instance, quite stupid. You've suffered a limiting injury and there's nothing shameful about giving yourself time to recover. If you can't afford to hire help, there are agencies—"

"I have a day woman, Mrs. Rosales, who cleans and fixes my three meals," she cut him off sharply. "And Edith Crum, the substitute teacher, was here until five o'clock."

"What about nights? You shouldn't be in this house alone. Can't Mrs. Difalco stay with you?"

"Angie has a husband and child." Gail gave him a patronizing smile. "Thank you for your concern. I do appreciate your interest, but I'm fine."

"Are you?"

Her bleak eyes met his steadily but her quickened breathing betrayed an inner tension ready to snap. Her courage and her dogged determination to handle things herself filled him with amazement. As the soft light of the lamp bathed her face, other less platonic emotions overtook him. She was so damned appealing that it was all he could do to keep from moving beside her on the couch.

"Gail, please, I want to help." He realized that his husky tone revealed more emotion than he had intended, so he added more briskly, "That's my job, you know."

She nodded. "I know... and I'm glad you came."

Her manner was still controlled, but as their eyes met, he felt her reaching out to him, wanting to find reassurance in his presence.

"I'm glad I came, too," he said with quiet honesty.

She took a deep breath. "I was sitting in the dark because..." She faltered.

"What it is, Gail?"

"I—I got another package." Her lower lip quivered.

Without even thinking, he was by her side in an instant. Gail's valiant effort to hide her fear crumbled. She turned to him with a silent plea for help in her stricken eyes. She didn't protest when he put an arm around her shoulders.

"Take it easy." Now he knew why she had been cowering in the dark like a hunted animal. Alarm stiffened the cords in his neck. The horrible shoe and note was not going to be an isolated incident as he had hoped. He knew with sickening certainty that Gail had become a target for malicious torment. There was no telling where it would lead. Thinking about all the crazies running loose sent a cold prickling up his spine. More than ever, he wanted to know why Lieutenant Lamont had reacted so strongly.

"It's all right," he soothed, brushing back hair that had drifted forward on her cheek. "We'll get to the bottom of this ugly business. I promise you." His husky voice betrayed the sudden desire he felt.

Impulsively he touched his lips to the top of her head as it lay against his chest. Sweet-scented hair and the warmth of her scalp teased his nostrils. He traced the soft curve of her cheek, threaded his fingers in wisps of hair curling over her ears and wondered what it would be like to know every inch of the sweet length of her body. As he held her, he murmured words that had no meaning except reassurance that she was safe.

She rested against him until her tremors ceased and then she drew away. For a moment, she avoided his eyes as if embarrassed by the way she had given in. Then she straightened her shoulders and gave him a wan smile. "I really had myself under control until you came."

He took her hand firmly in his. "I know. What was it this time?"

She firmed her chin. "I'll show you."

She reached for her cane and he helped her to her feet, keeping a guiding hand on her arm as they walked down the hall to the kitchen. Inside the door, she flipped on a kitchen light and then nodded to a trash can near the back door. A long narrow florist box stuck out of it.

Curtis walked across the large kitchen, pulled out the green box and opened it. Inside were roses. A half dozen of them. All black. All very, very dead. A white card with a verse printed in red crayon lay in the middle of them.

"Roses are black.
Blood is red.
My pain will be gone,
When you are dead."

The words jabbed Curtis like a knife. *When you are dead.* The malevolent threat leaped off the paper like a deadly thing ready to strike. The word *dead* had been underlined three times and the jagged red slashes of crayon made him sick to his stomach. This was no mischievous taunting, more the ugly product of a deranged mind. It was all he could do not to ram the whole thing back down in the trash.

He knew Gail was waiting for him to say something, so he turned around slowly. Carrying the box, he walked back to the table where she had eased down into one of the kitchen chairs.

"When did you get this?" he asked as he laid the box on the table.

"Mrs. Rosales found it on the porch when she was ready to leave after she fixed my dinner. She brought it in and I opened it after she'd gone."

"Any idea when it was left?"

"Had to be between the time I returned from therapy and Mrs. Rosales's departure a couple of hours later, about five-thirty. It wasn't on the porch when I came home about four. We didn't have anyone coming in for lessons today."

"I don't suppose you saw or heard anything."

"I was in the back of the house all the time."

He sighed. "Well, Lieutenant Lamont will want to take a look at this . . . as well as the shoe."

She sent him an anxious look. "I—I'm afraid that won't be possible. When I got home I looked in the wastepaper basket where Angie had dumped it yesterday." She gulped. "Mrs. Rosales put out all the trash for collection this afternoon."

Curtis cursed himself for not having had the foresight to take charge of the package yesterday. He forced a smile. "Well, no matter," he said, hoping to ease her discomfort. "But I think it's best that we call Lieutenant Lamont tonight and tell him about this."

She brushed a hand over her eyes and was silent for a moment. Then she nodded and said wearily, "I suppose so. I keep thinking this is all a bad dream that will go away if I ignore it."

Curtis wanted to take her in his arms again. She didn't deserve to suffer any more emotional abuse. He clenched his fists, wanting to vent his rage on the person responsible for such diabolical torment.

He strode over to the kitchen telephone and dialed a number. "Lieutenant? Curtis O'Mallory here. Sorry to bother you at home, but the client I told you about this afternoon has received another package...this time with a threat. I thought you ought to know."

Curtis listened, nodded, and then said, "Right. I'd appreciate it." He gave the policeman the address and then hung up.

He saw that Gail's face was white and her lips stiff. He sat down in a chair beside her at the table and reached over and took her hand. "The lieutenant will stop by in a few minutes. You'll like Jon Lamont. He was a good friend of my father's. They worked on some cases together before my father died a few years back."

Gail looked at him in surprise. "Your father was a policeman?"

"No, a lawyer. And my mother was a social worker. I guess I took after her. Decided to be a rehabilitation counselor. Gives me a reason to stick my nose in other people's business." Knowing her steely core of independence, he was prepared for open resentment that he had taken charge of the matter and called Lamont. He was relieved when she smiled back.

"You do it very well. And I do appreciate your coming over tonight...keeping me company." The lines in her face eased and her tone brightened. "Could I offer you something...a beer...hot chocolate?"

"A beer sounds good. How about you?" He was at the fridge before she could get up.

"There are glasses in the cabinet," she said as he set a couple of bottles of Coors on the table.

"I'm a bottle man myself."

"Me too." She laughed as if they had discovered an important likeness. "Pretzels?"

"Is there anything better with beer?"

As they sat at the round oak table, Curtis could see that Gail had incorporated the charm of the nineteenth-century kitchen with modern-day appliances and work savers. A lovely cherrywood cupboard was filled with porcelain dishware and copper utensils hung on racks near the electric stove. He could see a butler's pantry through a half-open door and a flight of stairs that must have been used by servants at one time.

"You love flowers, I see." He nodded at a small alcove that Gail had filled with plants. A desk faced the windows, and he could picture her sitting there writing or talking on the desk phone. "Makes a cozy corner," he said with approval.

His eyes traveled across the room to a back porch that might have been a scullery at one time, he decided. Now it seemed to serve as storage room and was filled with boxes.

Gail followed his gaze. "I was trying to sort out things that have accumulated for years. My aunt inherited the house through her husband's family. I think she was afraid to throw away a pincushion. I haven't begun to tackle the attic."

"It's a beautiful house," he complimented her. "I've always been partial to Old World stateliness."

They exchanged a few superficial comments about changing times, and with relaxed ease, they began to talk about their backgrounds. He learned that Gail had grown up in eastern Colorado and Curtis in Colorado Springs, a town ninety miles south of Denver. She'd graduated from the University of Colorado.

"I taught in the public schools until I started the Learning House," she told him. "Very boring life, I'm afraid."

"Any torrid romances?" he pried.

A flicker of shadow crossed her face. "Nothing permanent. I find it difficult not to be in the driver's seat all the time."

"So I've noticed," he said with a teasing grin.

"What about you?" she countered.

"I don't mind leaving the driving to someone else...if they don't run me into a telephone pole. Unfortunately, I made the mistake of marrying a gal who took me for a real ride...financially, that is. Three years ago, she dumped me for a wealthy surgeon. She'd been a client of mine, so I learned my lesson...never mix pleasure with business."

There was a sullen silence between them. Gail set down her drink and said steadily, "Very wise. Emotions can get out of hand, can't they?"

He felt her withdraw and was cursing himself for a fool when the doorbell rang. She stiffened.

"I'll let him in," said Curtis. Impulsively, he gave her shoulder a reassuring squeeze as he passed her chair.

Chapter Six

Curtis greeted the policeman at the front door. Lieutenant Lamont was a slightly built man in his forties whose black spectacles made him look more like a bookkeeper than a detective. Dark eyes snapped with energy and intelligence. He spoke in a soft, measured cadence unless he was riled—then his speech became as sharp as the jaws of a bear trap. With quick, purposeful steps, he walked with Curtis down the hall to the kitchen.

Gail stiffened against a nervous fluttering in her stomach as Curtis made the introductions. "Lt. Jon Lamont...Miss Gail Richards."

"Thank you for coming," she murmured, shaking his slender hand. Now that the detective was there, she felt a rising sense of guilt for presuming on his time. She was positive that he would think her some kind of neurotic. Why in heaven's name had she let Curtis talk her into it? She had always been a private person, determined to handle her own problems as best she could. She detested anyone poking and prying into her private affairs. The hospital experience was demoralizing enough, and now this.

"I convinced Gail that we ought to call you," said Curtis as if reading her thoughts. "Like the old adage says, better safe than sorry." He directed the last sentence at her, accompanied by a reassuring smile.

"Well, let's see what we have." Lamont examined the box of dead roses and held the card gingerly in his gloved hand as he read the printed message. Then he looked at the florist's name stamped on the box.

Gail couldn't tell from his neutral expression whether he was dismissing the whole thing as a juvenile prank or taking it seriously. She had the weird feeling that her own integrity was at stake in some way. She was moved to explain why he was in her kitchen looking at dead roses and reading a sickening rhyme. "This is the second thing that's been left."

"Yes, so Curtis told me. The more evidence we have, the better. Maybe we'll get something from the tennis shoe."

She sent Curtis a look of consternation and he said quickly, "I'm sorry, Lieutenant, by the time I told Gail you wanted to see everything, the housekeeper had dumped the box, shoe, note, everything in the trash. It was picked up sometime today."

The detective was not pleased.

"We didn't know that we might need it as evidence," explained Gail.

"I could have enlightened you . . . if you'd reported it." Lamont's eyes snapped.

Gail bristled at the unfair criticism. "I'm sorry, Lieutenant Lamont, but yesterday there didn't seem to be any reason to make a big deal out of it. I dismissed the whole thing as a sick joke." She met his eyes squarely. "I'm still not sure it's anything more than that. Curtis took it upon himself to inform you—"

"And I'm glad I did," Curtis countered. "I should have insisted yesterday. You can't deny that this second note takes it out of the fun-and-games category. Right, Lieutenant?"

"That's what I'm here to find out," he said curtly. He took out his notebook. "Now tell me where you found the packages."

"Both of them on the front porch." Gail gave him approximate times and he took down Angie's and Mrs. Rosales's names.

"Describe the tennis shoe. What did the note say?"

Curtis answered him succinctly and Gail had little to add. She hadn't looked at the bloody offering that closely, and she had tried to put the horrid rhyme out of her mind. She felt sick as Curtis recited it.

"Diddle, diddle dumpling, poor young John,
Killed in the street, his lifeblood gone.
One shoe off... and one shoe on,
Dead in the street, poor young John."

The lieutenant questioned her about the accident and the death of Johnnie Beeman. She answered all his questions but felt she had been of very little help. None of it made sense.

"Well, thank you, Miss Richards," said the lieutenant as if she'd been an entertaining hostess. He picked up the box of dead roses. "I'll have the lab check this over. Run some tests...fingerprints and the like, but I doubt that the perpetrator has any kind of a record. I'll check out the Beeman family and do a little snooping at the boy's school. Someone may talk."

"And in the meantime...?" prodded Curtis.

He paused and gave Gail a measuring look. "You live here alone, Miss Richards?"

She nodded. "Yes."

"Pretty big place for one person."

She resented his patronizing tone. What right did he have to question her life-style? She met his gaze squarely. "I've turned several downstairs rooms into my learning center. My living quarters are on the second floor... usually, that is."

He pushed back his glasses and waited for her to continue. For some reason she felt compelled to defend herself as if the detective was waiting to pounce on her decisions. A good technique for eliciting information, she thought, and she indicated her cane. "The stairs. For a few weeks I'm sleeping down here." She nodded toward the small back hall off the kitchen. "There's a small maid's room and half bath."

"Mind if I take a look." Without waiting for permission, he disappeared down the short back hall. They heard his quick footsteps as he checked out the bathroom and small bedroom. When he came back, he seemed satisfied. "A dead-end hall...that's good."

He walked through the kitchen and back porch and opened the door. A gust of cold air swept through the kitchen. "Do you always leave your doors unlocked?" he demanded when he came back to the table.

"I—I assumed Mrs. Rosales had locked it," she stammered.

"Don't assume anything," he ordered.

"I think Gail needs some protection," said Curtis. "Can't you assign a man to watch the house?"

Lamont's eyes narrowed as he peered through his glasses at Curtis. "Wish I could," he snapped. "But there's not enough provocation for the expense. We have hundreds of harassment cases every week. The department would be bankrupt if we assigned guards in every case." He turned to Gail. "You understand, Miss Richards, if anything further develops we will reassess the situation."

She nodded.

Curtis flushed with anger. "What you mean, if Gail is physically attacked, you'll protect her after the fact?"

"I agree with Lieutenant Lamont," said Gail quickly. "It would be ridiculous to make too much out of this. I'm embarrassed to have taken up your time, Lieutenant."

She stood up and turned to Curtis. "And I appreciate your concern, I really do. Thank you for coming over," she said in a tone of dismissal. "Now, I think I'll call it a day. If you don't mind seeing yourselves out..."

Lamont nodded. His expression softened slightly. "In most cases this kind of harassment usually turns out to be quite harmless."

"I understand," she said, but something in his tone detracted from his reassurance. *"In most cases."*

"Good night." Lamont spun on his heels and left.

"See you tomorrow," said Curtis, and she was startled when he kissed her lightly on the cheek. "Call me if you need to talk."

She was too flustered to respond and a little annoyed when the warmth on her cheek lingered long after he'd gone.

THE NEXT MORNING Gail waited for her housekeeper to come, but by nine o'clock, Mrs. Rosales still hadn't shown. The perky, energetic woman was scheduled to arrive at seven o'clock. Yesterday morning the kitchen had been filled with aromatic odors of coffee and fresh biscuits by the time Gail was ready for breakfast. In contrast, this morning the large kitchen remained silent and empty long after Gail had two cups of instant coffee and a slice of buttered toast.

Gail rated dependability as one of the most important traits a person could have. As a result, she was a little more than slightly irritated and disappointed when she went to the phone and called the Happy Household Service, the agency where Angie had engaged Mrs. Rosales.

"Oh, yes, Miss Richards," responded a pleasant smooth voice. "I was just about to call you. Unfortunately Mrs. Rosales called in sick this morning...something about tainted food."

"Oh, I'm sorry." Gail's irritation instantly vanished and she felt contrite. "I hope it isn't serious." Even though she'd only been there one day Gail had been relieved to have the pleasant Mexican woman assume responsibility for meals and cleaning.

"I'm sure she'll be back on the job very soon...and in the meantime, I'm sending a replacement... Inga Neilson. She's one of our most efficient young ladies. A very hard worker." She hesitated just slightly before she added, "Inga isn't quite as personable as Mrs. Rosales, but I know you'll be pleased with her dedication. I apologize for any inconvenience, Miss Richards. These things happen, you know."

Gail agreed and hung up, wondering why she felt uncomfortable with the change of housekeeper. After all, Mrs. Rosales had only been with her one day. This new woman would probably be just as good, and if she didn't like her, she could request someone else.

Maybe it was the sleepless night. Bone-deep fatigue. Or a growing apprehension that her life had somehow been caught in a vicious vise. Nothing seemed sure and ordinary anymore.

Unfortunately Gail found Inga Neilson's personality abrasive from the moment the young woman sauntered through the house, viewing the interior with a distasteful quiver of her nose. Somewhere in her twenties, she wore her ash blond hair pulled back tightly in a ponytail. She wore no makeup and her Nordic features were too heavy to be pretty. She was dressed in a denim jacket over a large brown sweatshirt and faded jeans.

Gail found herself apologizing for the oak flooring that needed to be swept and polished. She quickly assured Inga that she needn't concern herself with the classroom parlor or the littered library where reading instruction took place. From the way the Inga's eyes swept over intricately carved woodwork and door panels, Gail wondered if the young woman had ever been in a vintage house like this one. She stared at the furniture as if each piece was a monstrosity not to be believed.

"Mrs. Difalco will straighten up those rooms each day after afternoon classes."

In the kitchen Inga eyed Gail's dirty cup and saucer on the table and walked around the room, looking at each appliance as if deciding whether the model and make suited her fancy. She marched to the door of the cluttered back porch and stared at the mess for a brief moment before turning around and peering into the butler's pantry. When she opened the door to a servants' staircase that rose to the two floors above, Gail didn't bother to hide her irritation.

"We don't use those stairs anymore. You needn't bother with anything on the second floor. My room and bath are down the back hall. You're to do my rooms up everyday and prepare three meals before you leave at five." Gail's tone had become quite crisp and authoritarian. She fully expected the young woman to march out of the house without so much as a by-your-leave. Instead, she hung her jacket up on a peg near the back door.

"I'll do up the kitchen first." Her tone was a dismissal to Gail. She placed her hands on her hips, waiting.

"Fine," said Gail. "I'll have lunch at twelve."

More than once that morning Gail sensed a pair of ice-blue eyes boring into the back of her head. A quick turn of her head caught a disappearing glimpse of a ponytail.

About midmorning Gail went to her room to rest. She found the bed made up with hospital perfection and the bathroom smelling of antiseptic. All flowers on the dresser had been removed. Books and magazines had disappeared from her bedside and were in a drawer. The huge wardrobe had been dusted and all clothes put out of sight. Impersonal and stark, the small room had increased in ugliness. A penetrating coldness made Gail feel like an intruder in her own house. A feeling of dismay came over her.

"I'm just tired," Gail told herself as she lay down on the crisply made bed. "I hired the gal to clean and that's what she's doing." In spite of the mental lecture, she had difficulty dozing off into a fitful sleep that was reminiscent of the restless nights she'd spent in the hospital.

She came awake with a jerk. Someone's hand was on her shoulder. Arctic eyes stared down at her. A cold hard line defined unsmiling lips. Adrenaline lurched through Gail's body. This was no dream. Gail grasped her cane, and with a stab of pain, she sat up, ready to defend herself.

Inga glared at her.

Gail's body tensed, poised for danger.

"Lunch."

For a moment, Gail's mind didn't process the word. She stared at the young woman as if she had been speaking a foreign language.

Inga eyed the cane warily as if ready to jerk it out of Gail's hand. "You said you wanted to eat at twelve."

A mixture of relief, bewilderment and embarrassment swept over Gail. She swallowed hard and managed to say, "I guess I did oversleep."

The young woman's eyes flickered to the medicine bottle on the nightstand. Her mouth curled in a knowing smile. "Maybe you shouldn't take so many of them pills."

"I only take what is prescribed," Gail countered with a flash of irritation.

"Real easy to take an overdose. Lots of people do." For a moment a smile reached Inga's eyes. "You were groaning in your sleep, you know."

Gail had no way of knowing if the charge was true or false. The satisfied gleam in Inga's eyes told it was probably true. It was always demoralizing not to be in control of one's behavior at all times. Gail's resentment against the housekeeper mushroomed. She felt defensive and ill at ease in her own house.

"Thank you, Inga. I'll wash up and be right there," she said dismissively.

Inga left with an arrogant swing of her long ponytail. A few minutes later, Gail sat alone at the kitchen table, picking at a Caesar salad and a serving of canned peaches, while Inga moved about the kitchen, waiting pointedly to do up her lunch dishes.

The day before, Gail had eaten with Mrs. Rosales at the kitchen table, enjoying the light conversation about her five children and a pet magpie with a broken wing that had joined the family. There was no such lunchtime chatter with Inga Neilson. With relief, Gail finished most of her lunch and then made her escape to the library. A few minutes later Angie Difalco came in with a merry bustle, hanging on to her three-year-old son.

"What a morning! Jimmy decided to play with a broken bottle he found in the yard. Had to take him to the doc to have a three-inch cut sewed up."

The youngster grinned and held up his bandaged hand as if it was a trophy. His brown eyes twinkled. "I got ice cream."

Angie laughed. "Not a good reinforcement. I think I'm rewarding the wrong behavior."

Jimmy tugged free of his mother's hand and bounced around the room investigating everything within reach.

"Hasn't slowed him down much," Gail said with a chuckle, wishing she had a tenth of his energy.

"What's the matter, gal?" Angie asked quickly, seeing her wistful expression. "Aren't you feeling well? If you ask me, you're trying to do too much, too fast. Good heavens, it hasn't been a month since you were lying on an operating table. I think everyone's rushing you. All that physical therapy wears you out."

"Muscles will lose their tone and atrophy if not used."

"I still think you ought to take it easy for a few weeks. No need to push yourself to the brink of a nervous breakdown."

"I'm fed up with depending on other people for everything," Gail snapped.

"Doesn't hurt to let your friends offer a little help now and again. There's such a thing as being too proud, you know."

At Angie's chastising tone, Gail felt instantly contrite. "Sorry, I guess I'm just uptight, Angie. Mrs. Rosales is sick and the agency sent someone else in her place. I'm uncomfortable around the new woman. She's not very sociable."

"Are you hiring her to clean or be sociable?"

Leave it to Angie's practicality to put things in the right perspective, thought Gail, duly chagrined. "Maybe I am overreacting."

"It's time you had help taking care of this place," declared Angie. "You were doing too much before the accident. Now let me get things set up for Miss Crum. She's scheduled with Mr. Devitto this afternoon."

"You're one in a million," said Gail thankfully.

Angie gave a nonchalant wave of her hand. "You have a good afternoon but don't wear yourself out! As soon as I finish here, I'm going to run Jimmy over to nursery school and then I'll be back before the first student arrives at three-thirty." She spun around. "Jimmy? Jimmy! Now where is that kid?"

He wasn't in the library nor the adjoining living room. Swearing and yelling his name, Angie checked Gail's sitting room, the dining room and kitchen.

"Where is that little monster?" she said in an exasperated tone when she came back.

"Maybe Inga has seen him," offered Gail. "She is in the kitchen."

"No she isn't. I've been in every room on this floor."

Gail frowned. She was positive the woman hadn't left. "Then where . . . ?"

"Maybe the little rascal went upstairs," said his mother. She left the room and her steps sounded on the stairs, followed by muffled walking overhead. As she called Jimmy's name, her voice floated faintly down the stairs.

Gail left the library and walked back to the kitchen. She looked at the peg where Inga Neilson had hung her jacket. It was empty. Then she had gone, thought Gail angrily. Just like her to walk out without a word. Irresponsible, that's what she was!

Gail was about to turn around when she realized that the back door was slightly open. At the same time she heard Jimmy's squeal. Gail looked out the back porch window—and couldn't believe her eyes. The disagreeable housekeeper was playing in the snow with Jimmy. Her normal glowering visage had changed. The muscles in her face were relaxed, her mouth looked soft and full, and there was only tenderness in the way she embraced the child, tossing him in a playful fashion.

When she saw Gail standing in the doorway watching, she stiffened. Her expression became wooden as if a mask had been suddenly drawn over her features.

"Jimmy's mother is looking for him," said Gail. The woman's contradictory behavior made her uneasy.

Inga set the boy down and Jimmy ran to the house. Gail didn't look back at the housekeeper as she took the boy's hand and led him back to his mother.

Angie wasn't disturbed at all, and Gail didn't know why her heart was racing in such a fashion. There was nothing sinister about the incident. Obviously Inga liked children better than adults. Nothing ominous about that.

Angie left and Miss Crum arrived a short time later. Gail would have liked to talk to her about Mr. Devitto's progress, but she knew that the opinionated teacher would consider it interference. The bouncy plump lady was pleasant enough, smiling and chatting about her love of teaching, but there was something rather flat in her pretty blue eyes.

Gail quickly retreated to her sitting room until she saw the Ambu-Cab drive up. She went out the front door and was cautiously making her way down the porch steps when she stopped. Something gray was crumpled in the snow near the bottom step.

Her stomach turned over in revulsion.

A dead cat. Its neck was twisted at an ugly angle and a limp tongue hung out of its mouth. Glassy eyes, wide in death, stared up at her.

Chapter Seven

Curtis struggled to keep his mind on the endless paperwork the State of Colorado required on every rehabilitation client. He kept glancing at his watch, knowing that Gail's therapy session was scheduled for two-fifteen. When he thought about her, his usual efficient handling of client problems deserted him. The remembrance of her soft skin as his mouth brushed her cheek stirred a longing involving his deepest emotions. She had been in his thoughts during a restless night, and he'd even tried to call her first thing when he arrived at the office, but her line had been busy.

Last night, when he had walked with Lamont out to his car, he had fired a volley of questions at the detective. "You've had another case like this, haven't you, Lamont?"

"There are some similarities," he had answered curtly.

"Like what?" Curtis's brisk tone matched his.

"Nursery rhyme threats...ugly innuendos...broken dolls and the like."

"And what happened?"

The lieutenant shoved back his glasses without answering and then opened his car door.

Curtis grabbed his arm. "This other victim... what happened to her?"

"She OD'd on drugs. Sherrie Sinclair...sixteen years old. Had been shooting up for a couple of years."

Curtis frowned. "I don't understand."

"About three months before Sherrie died, she backed out of a driveway when she was high on something and ran over a kid on a tricycle. A judge gave her probation on the condition she complete a drug rehabilitation program. According to the mother, right after the accident ugly packages started coming...all with nursery rhymes that taunted her with the child's death. They kept coming until the night she was found dead of an overdose in her car. Her mother blames the repugnant harassment for her suicide." Lamont peered through his glasses at Curtis. "How stable is Gail Richards? Is she likely to cave in under this kind of torment?"

Curtis weighed his answer. He knew that humans were like volatile substances: once an emotional flashpoint was reached they could explode. Heaven knows, Gail had suffered enough physical trauma to weaken her emotional strength, but having glimpsed the uncompromising nature of her personality, he believed that she would fight to the last ounce of her being before she would crumble. "Gail is the most determined, courageous woman I've ever met."

Lamont raised an eyebrow, gave a knowing snort and climbed in his car. Before he closed the door, he growled. "Let's hope you're right."

THINKING BACK over the conversation, Curtis was positive that he had been right in reassuring Lamont that Gail had the inner strength to see her through the malicious torment.

His secretary, Myra, came in with a stack of letters. "Sorry to disturb you. From that frown I'd guess you're having one of those days."

Curtis gave her a smile. "Not really. Just thinking long, long thoughts."

"I have that data processing seminar over the lunch hour," she reminded him. "I'll probably be gone a couple of hours."

He nodded. "I plan to be in the office most of the day."

"I was surprised to see your car in Miss Richards's driveway last evening. And another one parked in front. Was she having some kind of welcome-home party?" Her tone accused him of somehow having been remiss for not keeping her informed.

Curtis hated Myra's proprietary attitude toward his personal life. This wasn't the first time she'd let him know that she was well aware of his activities outside the office. More than once she'd shown up at some gathering where he happened to be and she was always dropping casual remarks to show she knew he'd been out on a date. He wasn't in the mood for her possessive curiosity, so he gave his attention to the papers without answering.

Myra shuffled uncomfortably. "I have a friend who lives in one of the high-rise apartments down the street and I pass that old house a lot. I wasn't checking up on you."

"I'm glad." He handed back the papers and met her gaze directly.

A flush crept up in her throat. "No need to get testy."

She picked up the signed letters, spun on her high heels and left.

WHEN LARRY WHEELED Gail toward the therapy department a little after two o'clock, she tried to put aside the lingering repulsion at finding a dead cat on her doorstep. Since there hadn't been another note, she couldn't decide whether the animal carcass was another malicious act or just an ugly coincidence. In any case, nothing could be done about it, she reminded herself, and purposefully put it out of her mind for the time being.

Just as they reached the door of the P.T. department, an attractive woman with blue eyes and auburn hair too perfect to be natural was just coming out a door of the water therapy room. Her expression tightened for a moment and then smoothed.

"Hi, Myra," Larry greeted her. "How come you're dressed up like a gorgeous doll today? Oh, I know. That downtown seminar. Whatcha doing back so soon?"

"It got over early."

"Jeez, how do you expect anyone to keep his mind on business when you look like that?" His eyes flickered appreciatively over a royal blue sweater the color of her eyes.

Gail could tell the woman was pleased that Larry had noticed her appearance, but she pointedly ignored him and gave her attention to Gail. "You must be Miss Richards. I'm Myra Monet, Mr. O'Mallory's secretary. Since I had a little time, I thought I'd drop by and introduce myself. I like to put faces to names of our clients." She gave Gail a look that went beyond casual interest.

More like a tailor taking mental measurements, thought Gail. Myra's dress and manner hardly fitted the secretary stereotype. She felt a twinge of envy that this attractive woman had the pleasure of Curtis's company day in and day out. "I'm glad to meet you," Gail responded politely.

"Likewise. Every case that comes through our office is very interesting. Unfortunately, we have a lot of accident victims in our rehab programs. Some are left with permanent disabilities." Myra's smile dismissed Gail's condition as one of their minor cases. "Mr. O'Mallory works very hard to get each one back to a productive life. Haven't you found him to be very personable and encouraging?"

"He's been very helpful," Gail responded in a neutral tone. "Do you find him personable as an employer?"

The change of direction in the conversation was not to Myra's liking. She tried for a smile and came up with a feeble "Nice to have met you. Well, I have to get back to the office. We're swamped with new cases. Every one of them wanting special attention."

Larry had been taking in the exchange with an amused glint in his eyes. "Well, ladies, I'd better get Miss Richards into therapy or Beth will have my head," Larry said. "She hates to get off schedule."

Myra gave him a patronizing smile. "You can relax, Larry. Beth went down the hall to make a telephone call. I'm sure Gail won't mind waiting." Her laugh was pointed. "Every attractive gal thinks that the whole place should revolve around her. It's a low blow when she discovers that it doesn't."

Larry seemed uncomfortable as he pushed the wheelchair past Myra. "Don't mind her, Miss Richards," he said in a confidential tone. "Myra's got a thing for her boss. Everyone knows it." He winked. "And you're prettier than most."

As they approached the therapy tank, Roberta Benson was getting some equipment out of a lower cupboard and when she heard Larry's remarks, she straightened up. "Your gossiping tongue is going to land you in big trouble someday, Larry," she flared. "I ought to report you."

Larry just grinned back at her. "But you won't, will you, Bobbie, dear?" He tipped his blond head at a cocky angle and waited.

"Someday..." She swore under her breath and brushed past him into the other room.

Larry chuckled. "Poor gal. Roberta's one of those man-haters who's always looking under her bed— hoping to find Tom Cruise hiding there."

His tone made Gail wonder if Roberta might have found a good-looking orderly near her bed at some point. Larry promised to be back after her session and started out the door just as Beth came back.

Beth ignored his quip about sneaking off for an unscheduled break. Her mind was obviously elsewhere as she readied Gail for therapy. Gail missed Beth's easy, homey chatter of the day before but any attempts to start a conversation with her failed. The aide moved about the room in a mechanical fashion and only gave a curt nod in reply to Gail's remarks. Curly sandy hair had escaped from her headband and her white slack suit was full of wrinkles as it stretched tightly over her ample buttocks and thighs.

Too bad, thought Gail. Beth might be quite pretty if she lost that husky girl-from-the-farm look. Obviously, she was having a bad day, thought Gail. *Well, aren't we all?* A deep weariness suddenly overtook her. Maybe she could restore some of her vitality by moving her arms and legs lazily about in warm water.

Beth tightened the straps holding Gail's hips on the canvas stretcher, then moved to the controls at the head of the tank. With a rather preoccupied expression, she turned a dial and the stretcher began to lower. Unlike at the previous session, the stretcher didn't stop just below the surface but kept going down and down until Gail's face was several inches underwater.

As the water poured over her face, Gail tried to sit up but couldn't. Her chest was firmly strapped down. Screams tore from her throat. She arched her head, gasping and choking as water poured into her mouth. She flailed her arms. Kicked her feet. Her hands clawed at the straps, trying to find the buckles.

I'm going to drown.

As raw panic surged through her, the stretcher gave a shudder and rose. Water poured off her face. Choking, she gasped for air. In the middle of a coughing spasm she felt strong hands loosening the confining belts. Larry helped her sit up.

"It's okay," he soothed as she gulped air. Water from Gail's drenched hair flowed down over her face.

Beth was hysterical. "The switch stuck...the switch stuck. Oh, my God! My God!"

"Stop it, Beth! Get some towels!" Larry snapped. "Oh, I'm so sorry," wailed Beth. She wrapped Gail in a large towel and began to roughly dry her. "The damn control stuck. I kept trying—"

"You should have gotten her up immediately. Not fooled around trying to get the switch to work. If I hadn't happened by—"

"I wouldn't have let her drown," sobbed Beth. "She was only under a few seconds. Besides, the switch was working perfectly just before noon."

"We're going to have to report this, you know," Larry said firmly.

Beth covered her face with her hands and began to cry.

WHEN MYRA CAME BACK to the office a half hour later, there was suppressed excitement in her dark blue eyes. Curtis couldn't help teasing her. "Myra, only you could find computer software exciting. I bet everybody else was half-asleep most of the session."

"There's nothing wrong with learning how to do a better job," she countered in a belligerent tone. "I know that some women are content to slide along. Not me. I don't like being at the bottom of the heap—in anything.''

''No one can be good at everything,'' he said evenly. ''We all have to make compromises.''

Her dark eyes flared with anger and Curtis quickly tried to defuse it. ''But if anyone can set a pace, it's you, Myra. And I appreciate the efficient way you handle things around here. If you decided to move up into the State office, I'll give you a glowing recommendation.''

''Are you trying to get rid of me?''

''Not at all. I just think you should be rewarded for your dedication.'' Then he stood up and said casually, ''I think I'll stretch my legs. I want to talk to someone in P.T.''

''Gail Richards?'' Myra demanded, the excited glint back in her eyes.

He nodded.

A smile tugged at the corner of her lips. ''One of the office girls just told me there'd been an accident in P.T. Something went wrong with the switch on the tank. Gail Richards was the patient involved.''

Curtis was on his feet in an instant. When he reached the water therapy room, Larry was there with an electrician who was working on the tank's control panel.

''Hi, Mr. O'Mallory,'' greeted Larry, obviously ready to relate the exciting happening to another receptive ear. ''Lucky I was hanging around in the hall, just outside the door, talking to the cute little number who works in the lab... you know that pretty silver-haired blonde? Anyway, I thought I heard a funny gasp and then an unusually loud splash when the stretcher hit the water." He straightened his shoulders. "I thought I'd better check it out."

He waited for Curtis's nod of approval before he continued. "The patient was submerged and Beth was frantically trying to work the Lift control. Miss Richards was beating the water with her arms and legs but the straps wouldn't let her sit up. She might have drowned if I hadn't gotten her out of there in two shakes."

Curtis addressed a question to the maintenance man. "How could this have happened?"

He shrugged. "This unit is about eight years old. I'm not surprised it went on the fritz."

"Beth is really upset. She's in the lounge crying her eyes out." Larry gave Curtis a reassuring smile. "But no harm done."

I wonder. A worried frown creased his forehead.

"Accidents do happen," said Larry.

"Yes"... *but not always to the same person.*

When he hurried through the door of the exercise room, Scuffy corralled him. "Miss Richards got drowned in the tank."

"Scuffy!" Roberta was working with the child on the exercise table next to Gail's. "Keep your mind on your exercises. Now, pay attention."

Curtis bent over Gail. Her hair was still wet, her face pale, and her smile was wan. He took her hands in his. "Are you all right?"

She nodded.

Anger, relief, fear and a mixture of indefinable emotions washed over him. "What happened?"

"I—I don't know. Something went wrong...with the controls. The stretcher went all the way under. I was strapped down...and couldn't get up." Her lips quivered.

Blast it all, he swore silently. He swung around, wanting to vent his anger on somebody. "How did it happen, Roberta?"

"One of the controls shorted out, I guess." She obviously didn't want to discuss it. Her eyes warned Curtis to quit asking questions. "Now, Scuffy, swing that leg from the hip and tighten the muscles on the outside of your leg. That's better. See, you don't have to use the scissorlike gait."

Curtis turned back to Gail. "Is there anything I can do?"

Just be there for me. He had become an anchor in a situation where everything was suddenly dangerously out of balance. If she had been physically fit she would have dismissed the dunk under the water as a scary experience but nothing more. Weeks of pain and weakness had snapped her resiliency.

Curtis drove her home. His calm manner had helped put the unfortunate incident in proper perspective. The switch failure had been a fluke...and she just happened to be the unlucky one. She had regained her normal composure, but he searched her face as if trying to peer beneath the surface. "You're not going to let this cut down your physical therapy, are you?"

"Of course not," she bristled. "I have every intention of continuing the prescribed therapy as vigorously as possible."

"Good."

She thought his smile held a hint of relief as he pulled into her driveway. Several cars were parked out in front. Thank goodness some of her students had showed up for their lessons, thought Gail. She'd worked hard to build up her enrollment, and it frightened her to think of starting over again. As soon as her therapy sessions left her with any energy at all, she would resume teaching. As it was, she'd have to depend on Miss Crum for a few more weeks.

"I won't come in, then," said Curtis as he walked with her to the front door.

Gail didn't insist. She'd already felt guilty for imposing on him as much as she had. Myra's nettled remark echoed in her ears. *"I think it's a shame the way some clients impose on Curtis."* She stiffened against his guiding touch as he held the front door open for her.

"Call me if you need to talk."

"I will," she said, but she knew she wouldn't. His responsibility was to arrange for vocational rehabilitation. Nothing more.

"Gail . . . ?"

"Yes?" She forced an edge of impatience into her tone. She made her eyes bland as she looked at him.

"Nothing." He turned away.

She closed the door and leaned up against it for a moment to get her emotions back under control.

"I thought that might be you," said Angie, hurrying down the hall. She jerked her head toward Gail's sitting room. "There's someone waiting for you. A woman. Wouldn't tell me her business. Said it didn't have anything to do with arranging lessons. She's as jumpy as a cricket on a hot plate, if you ask me." Angie frowned. "You look beat. Want me to get rid of her?"

"Did she gave a name?"

"Sinclair... doesn't ring a bell with me," said Angie. "Never saw her before."

Gail sighed. "Tell her I'll see her but I'd sure like a cup of tea...and a couple of aspirin. You'll never guess what happened to me today."

"Nothing good, I can tell that."

"I'll tell you later. Right now, I just want to collapse in an easy chair. Everything's under control?" She gave a nod toward the reading rooms.

"Fine. Miss Crum's working with Mr. Devitto and I have Keith on some of the machines. Go get off your feet."

When Gail came into the sitting room, her visitor was standing at one of the side windows, staring outside. At the sound of Gail's cane, she jerked around. She was somewhere in her forties, her hair was an uncertain grayish blond and her stylish beige suit couldn't disguise a figure falling to middle-aged thickness. "Miss Richards?"

At Gail's nod she came forward, offering a hand with manicured nails. "I apologize for this intrusion, but I simply could not pass up the chance to talk with you. Not after that detective came around yesterday, trying to find a connection between you and Sherrie. You understand, don't you?''

"I'm afraid I don't," said Gail wearily. "Please sit down, Mrs. Sinclair. I've just returned from Crestview and I'm quite tired."

"Yes, of course. Again, I apologize."

Gail hoped that the woman would take the hint and state her business quickly, but she didn't. She was still rambling in an incoherent fashion when Angie brought in the tea and aspirin and raised her eyebrows at Gail as she left. It was several minutes later when Gail finally got the drift of what the woman was saying. A shock like that from a live wire went through Gail. "Your daughter ran over a child?"

"It wasn't Sherrie's fault. The little boy rode the tricycle right behind the car as she was backing out of our driveway. I know she shouldn't have been smoking pot, but she wasn't a killer, Miss Richards. And those horrible packages kept coming. It was awful. Sherrie was afraid to open the door, look in her locker or drive her car. She kept finding repugnant things and horrible rhymes accusing her of being a child killer." Mrs. Sinclair's eyes grew misty with tears.

Gail reached over and touched her hand. "I'm so sorry."

"After the tragedy, the judge put Sherrie on probation and sentenced her to enter drug rehabilitation. And my daughter straightened up. You have to believe me." Mrs. Sinclair's lips quivered. "They said Sherrie went back on drugs and gave herself an overdose, accidentally or deliberately—but I know she didn't." She straightened her shoulders. "I came to warn you, Miss Richards."

A spiderlike chill crept up Gail's spine.

"Somebody killed my daughter. The same somebody that sent her all those vicious things."

Chapter Eight

The noises began that night. At first Gail thought it was the squeak of the old bed that had disturbed her restless sleep, but as she lay still, suddenly wide-awake, she heard the muffled noise again. She stiffened, holding her breath. A faint crackling like quiet footsteps echoed on the floor above. Her heartbeat quickened and her mouth went dry. It sounded as if someone was stealthily moving about in one of the second-floor rooms. But no, it couldn't be. She was certain that everything had been locked up when Inga Neilson left after supper cleanup. *Easy,* she cautioned herself. Sounds were deceptive at night, especially in an old house like hers with its creaking boards, groaning pipes and settling walls.

She sent a nervous glance at the clock. Ten minutes past one. She had taken a pain pill several hours earlier, but her back muscles were still tensely knotted. With her eyes wide open, she lay stiffly in the bed without moving. She didn't want to miss the muffled sound if it came again. As the seconds passed, she began to reassure herself. All she could hear was a faint rustling of branches outside the small window and the scraping of a piece of metal on the roof. The wind must have come up, she reasoned. If she'd been up in her own room, she would easily have sorted out the sounds, knowing which were usual in the old house and identifying any strange ones, but being in an isolated room at the back of the house gave her a different perspective.

She waited uneasily.

Silence.

She began to breathe more deeply. Just a case of nerves, she thought, cautiously turning over in bed so she could sleep on her stomach. The loud squeak of the iron bed frame and springs was reassuring, and she felt foolish for giving way to nighttime jitters. She patted the pillow and thought about Curtis. She pictured his strong features and the distinguishing slivers of gray in his wavy dark hair. Not only was he one of the most attractive men she'd ever met, but she'd never been around someone so poised, professional and yet sensitive. She wondered what it would be like to have a man like that lying beside her in the night. She remembered the warmth of his lips on her cheek. If only they had met under different circumstances. She wanted to attract his interest at her best—not at her worst. His attentiveness under the circumstances might be tainted with pity. She couldn't stand it if he were just feeling sorry for her. If only—

The rest of the musing was cut off by a loud thud that echoed through the house. It sounded as if something had been knocked over. Gail was confused as to where the noise had come from. Upstairs or somewhere on the ground floor? She couldn't tell. She waited. Another muffled sound reached her ears. All doubt fled.

Someone was in the house.

A burglar? After her precious computers? She knew that such possessions were ripped off every day. Maybe burglars had been casing the house—knowing she was alone. The loss of her teaching equipment would be disastrous, but she knew better than to confront any intruders herself. She had to get to a phone and call 911.

Reaching for her cane, she stood up, wincing from a shooting pain down her back. The reality of her physical limitations swept over her. She'd always been quick and sure in her movements and physical activity of any kind had been a joy, but the accident had changed all that. Instead of being light, her steps were slow and labored as she made her way down the back hall to the kitchen. The tapping of her cane against the floor sounded loudly in her ears and heralded her movement as clearly as the beat of drumsticks.

The phone was in the recessed corner of the kitchen where Gail had placed a small desk in an alcove of flowers and plants. Only filtered moonlight came through kitchen windows. Cupboards and kitchen appliances were lost in possessive darkness, but the familiar hum of the refrigerator was reassuring. No furtive sounds reached Gail's ears as she paused for a moment in the doorway.

She took a step forward into the kitchen and then stopped abruptly. Her breath caught. A play of shadows near the butler's pantry brought a rise of cold fear. Was that a wavering figure pressed against the wall?

Gail gripped the cane head with a sweaty hand, straining her ears. Imperceptibly the impression faded and then disappeared all together. Strength flowed back into her watery legs. *An illusion.* She chided herself for behaving like a child making boogeymen out of shadows.

The hanging plants in the alcove made weird shadows against the windowpanes as she made her way around the kitchen table and chairs. She was trembling when she reached the phone sitting on her desk by the window and dialed the emergency number.

Her call was answered immediately. Gail croaked in a whisper, "A burglar...in my house."

"Your address, name, please." The female dispatcher's voice was quiet, smooth and authoritative.

Gail gave the information, trying to control a mounting panic as her ears picked up a hollow sound that seemed to be coming through the walls around her.

"Please stay on the line," the dispatcher ordered. "A car will be there in a few minutes. Don't do anything. Be calm...and stay on the phone. Understand?"

"Yes."

A few minutes? An eternity! *Please hurry...hurry!*

Gail cowered back against the wall, half-hidden in the midst of leaves and greenery that sat on shelves and hung from hooks near the windows. With every sense quivering like an antenna reaching out for any sound, movement or smell, she waited, muscles tensed. She kept a firm grip on the handle of her cane, her eyes sweeping every part of the kitchen that she could see. Someone could be moving toward her, and she wouldn't be able to see the intruder until he stood in front of her. She considered turning on a small desk lamp but feared it would only make her more vulnerable to anyone coming in the kitchen.

The reassuring voice of the operator was a lifeline to safety. Gail had begun to relax slightly when the long tendrils of a spider plant moved slightly above her head. At the same time, a draft of cold air had hit her legs.

She gasped.

"What's wrong? Are you all right?" demanded the dispatcher.

Gail couldn't answer until she swallowed hard to get some moisture in her mouth. "I think . . . someone might have gone out the back door," she whispered.

"Don't panic. Two officers will be there momentarily."

Gail strained to hear the high-pitched shrill of a siren. "I don't hear them."

"Their car is approaching your street . . . no siren. The officers will check the premises before they enter the house. Just wait. Stay on the line. Don't do anything."

The warning was really unnecessary, thought Gail, remaining pressed against the wall in the midst of her plants. Her present physical condition put a rein on any impulsive heroics. Not like a year ago when a punk kid had tried to steal her purse and she'd swung around and hit him so hard in the Adam's apple that he'd fled holding his throat and gasping for breath. Now, waiting there in the darkness, Gail rebelled against the helplessness, the agonizing wait, not knowing if her house was being stripped while she cowered in a corner of her own house.

"The officers are circling the house," the dispatcher related in a tone she might have used in making a commentary on some ordinary activity.

Thank heavens, Gail breathed.

"They will be coming in the house shortly."

It was an agonizing five minutes before Gail heard the back door open and a moving circle of light glittered on the kitchen floor.

"Police," announced a firm voice, and a second later the kitchen light came on.

Gail hung up the phone without thinking. She stepped out of the alcove. The two young officers who had answered her call looked like grown-up Boy Scouts, thought Gail, smart and trim in their uniforms and looking young enough to go off to camp.

"What happened, ma'am?" asked the tallest one, a sandy-haired, clean-cut fellow with slightly crooked teeth. His rather uncomfortable expression made her realize that she was only clad in a short brushed wool gown, barefoot and weaving slightly.

The second officer, dark-haired and stocky, asked, "Are you all right?"

She sat down in a kitchen chair before answering. "Yes."

"I'm Officer Kline," said the lanky young man. "This is Officer Mantelli. Tell us what happened."

Gail gripped her hands firmly in her lap. The pain of her nails biting her flesh seemed to steady her. "I heard noises . . . like someone was in the house. I was afraid someone was stealing my computers . . . in the front room."

"Stay here, ma'am. We'll check it out. Let's go, Mantelli."

Both men held their guns in a ready position as they eased out of the kitchen. Gail could hear them moving cautiously around the front of the house. Hugging herself, she tried to control a bone-deep chill that was a combination of fright and wearing only a scanty nightgown.

When nothing happened after several minutes of waiting, Gail's uneasiness began to be replaced by a feeling of foolishness. She was acting like an idiot. Returning to her bedroom, she put on a soft terry robe and her slippers. Filled with impatience and a need to know the worst, she made her way down the hall to the front of the house.

"Anything missing, ma'am?" asked Officer Mantelli, coming up behind her as she surveyed the front room. All the computers and reading machines were in place.

"Not that I can see."

"No sign of forced entry. Did the noises come from the front of the house?" he asked Gail.

"I'm not sure. There was a loud thud . . . like something dropped. And before that, I thought I heard someone walking upstairs." She moistened her dry lips. "And while I was waiting for you to come, there was a kind of scurrying coming through the walls."

"Like mice?" Officer Kline gave his crooked-toothed grin.

Gail could tell from their expression that they had already categorized this call "nervous woman hears mice in the walls and calls police."

She waited for them in the kitchen while they checked the second-floor rooms and the attic. They came back down to the kitchen by way of the servants' stairs.

"Anything?" she asked, knowing what their answer would be.

"Has anyone been upstairs lately?" asked the lanky officer.

"No. I've been sleeping downstairs since my accident."

"There were footprints in the dusty halls and stairs... even up to the attic," Kline began. "Are you sure that no one—"

And then Gail remembered. "Oh, I forgot. My teaching assistant was up there looking for her little boy."

He nodded. "Well, we didn't find anything else. You really should lock up, ma'am. Unlocked doors just invite trouble," lectured Mantelli as he smoothed a budding mustache.

"My doors *were* locked."

The officers exchanged patient looks. "When we arrived the back door was unlocked."

"I'm sure my housekeeper locked it before she left and..." Gail stopped. Last evening, she'd been sitting at the kitchen table and had just nodded when Inga asked if she wanted her to lock up. Gail knew the housekeeper had gone to the back door, but maybe she hadn't actually turned the lock. Maybe Inga had left it unlocked. "While I was waiting for you, I felt a draft—as if someone had gone out the back door," she admitted.

"Do you live alone, Miss Richards?"

"Yes." She was sensitive to his judgmental tone.

"Who else has a key to your house?"

"My teaching assistant has a key to the front door... but not the back. No one else."

"Have you ever lost a key and had to replace it?"

"No."

Officer Kline made notes in his notebook and then closed it. He cleared his voice as if not quite sure how he should handle the situation. "I don't doubt that you heard something, ma'am. But this is a big house." He shook his head. "Lots of things could have made a noise that might have startled you."

Mantelli eyed her cane. "I bet you're taking medicine to help things along."

The two men stood there looking at her in a way that fired Gail's temper. A legion of emotions had assaulted her since the accident—fear, apprehension, dread, panic and shock. She knew she was under great stress, but her senses were all intact. She was not imagining anything, but she knew it wouldn't do any good to argue with them. The officers had searched the house and found nothing. She drew herself up. "Thank you for your prompt response."

"If anything else develops, be sure and call in."

"Yes, I will."

They hastily made their exit from the house, insisting that Gail lock the back door behind them. She leaned her forehead against the cold pane of glass. *Don't let go. Don't let go,* a stern inner voice admonished her. Undoubtedly paranoia could make a breeze into a hurricane if she let it. More than ever she needed to keep her imagination under control. Despite the lecture, she couldn't dismiss the feeling that she was about to be assaulted by an evil force that could invade the sanctuary of her home at will.

THE WOMAN'S HOUSE was dark when she pulled her car into the driveway and unloaded the bulky object from her trunk. A cold wind whipped her hair and chilled her face, but an inner warmth and excitement sluiced through her veins, beading sweat on her palms. She felt new power and a sense of release from the torment that drove her. Like a victor returning with spoils, she carried into her house the stolen object, the symbol of her domination, the promise of just retribution when the time came.

The prize had been unexpected. She had simply been familiarizing herself with the house, deciding on the best means to dispense justice, searching for new ways of torment while she decided what kind of death would befall this killer of the innocent. There would be no sense of peace until she had laid her plans.

The size of the house had at first dismayed her, but delight soon followed. Secure in the knowledge that the injured woman would not be wandering about on the upper floors, she had moved stealthily up the stairs, the soft carpet muffling her steps and cool musty air touching her face.

Her bitterness had been fired by the valuable furnishings of the spacious bedrooms, but she was not tempted to take anything—not until she surveyed the attic. When her flashlight had traveled over the stored furniture, nothing had attracted her interest until the radius of light had played upon the old-fashioned cradle.

In her haste to get to it, she knocked over an iron floor lamp. The noise had sounded like the strike of a blacksmith's hammer. She grabbed up her treasure and quickly made her way down a flight of back stairs, but just as she had stepped through into the kitchen, she heard a tapping cane and footsteps, and had pulled back against the wall just in time. Retreating a few steps back up the staircase, she waited until she heard the dial of a telephone and a hoarse whisper.

Cursing the creaking sounds of her weight on the old boards, she left the stairway and hurried across the kitchen and made her way out the way she had entered—through the back door. The new key had worked fine.

A gleeful laugh accompanied her light steps across her small living room, up the stairs and down a hall leading to a back room. Before turning on the light, she set her booty down in the middle of the floor. Then she flipped the switch, stood back.

"It's all yours, Robbie," she said. Then she knelt on the floor by the empty cradle and began to rock it, singing softly, "Lullaby and good night...."

Chapter Nine

As soon as the policemen left, Gail called Curtis. She rationalized that the need to talk to him was a professional one. He was her rehab counselor and she had promised that she would call him night or day if she needed to talk. She expected his voice to be foggy with sleep at one o'clock in the morning, but she could tell from his resonant hello that he was wide-awake.

"Curtis...it's Gail. I'm sorry to bother you." She forced a light tone. "I've had a little excitement. The police were just here and..."

"The police? What happened? Are you all right?"

She had to reassure him several times that she was fine before he slowly released his breath and said evenly, "Tell me what happened?"

"I was asleep...but not too soundly. At first I didn't know what had wakened me. Then I heard some overhead noises. Muffled sounds like floorboards squeaking and quiet footsteps. But even as I listened, the only thing I could hear was the sound of the wind. I had just about convinced myself it was my imagination when I heard a thud. There was no doubt in my mind this time. So I called 911." She was pleased to find her voice full and even. "A couple of policemen came and checked it out. They didn't find anything." She gave a little self-mocking laugh. "I was sure that burglars were carrying out my computers. But nothing is gone."

"I'll be right over—"

"No," she said sharply. "Please, don't." She found it difficult enough maintaining her composure just hearing his voice. She knew that if he came to the house, she would want to be close to him, feel his hand in hers and lean into his protective warm embrace. She had too much pride to give in to the physical attraction that was growing stronger every time they were together. "I just want to talk."

He was silent for a moment and then agreed. "Perhaps you're right."

They talked for almost an hour. *He's a good counselor,* Gail thought. He was nondirective, allowing the conversation to flow easily from her own needs. She told him about the visit she'd had from Sherrie Sinclair's mother, and he admitted that he had learned about the case from Lieutenant Lamont. "I didn't think it would do any good to have you worrying about it. The girl was into heavy drugs."

"Her mother said she'd been straight since the accident."

"Every day is a struggle for an addict. Something must have happened to make her shoot up again. Sad case. I'm glad you're able to take everything in stride and look at coincidences for what they are."

"Sometimes I wonder." She mentioned the dead cat. "At first I was really shaken. Ready to believe it had been deliberately left there—even without a note."

She knew he was restraining himself when he responded in a deeper tone. "You didn't tell me about that."

"Angie had Mr. Devitto dispose of it. We decided some kids must have tossed it there."

"Maybe. Is it all right if I tell Lamont about it?" Curtis had learned to consult her before taking any action. She was one independent woman.

"If you think it's important," she said with open skepticism.

"I'll call him first thing in the morning. Are you sure you're going to be all right the rest of the night?"

"Of course."

He hesitated and then firmed his voice. "Gail, maybe you should consider taking a small apartment in one of the buildings closer to Crestview. You know, just for the time being. Until you get your strength back."

"Do you really think that would stop someone intent on tormenting me?" she asked bluntly.

"I honestly don't know, but your being alone in that big house at night worries me. If some psychopath is wandering in and out at will, you'd be better off living in an apartment where you're closer to other people."

"I'm not letting anyone drive me out of my home!" she flared. Anger instantly fused with a sense of utter frustration. "Besides, I'm not sure that someone was really in the house tonight. My imagination could be fueling a stupid paranoia brought on by a couple of malicious pranks. I guess that's why I called you...to reassure myself that I'm not going off the proverbial deep end. Calling the police like that and everything. You don't think I'm some kind of nut, do you?''

He chuckled. ''Only if a stubborn, self-directed, utterly charming woman can be classified as a nut.'' Then his tone softened. ''You have my reassurance, dear lady, that you are probably one of the most clearheaded women I have ever known.'' He hesitated. ''And one of the most attractive, I might add.''

She silently laughed at that. Attractive? It was a good thing he couldn't see her with her hair shooting out in all directions, wearing a flannel granny gown and an old robe. A man as good-looking as he was must be accustomed to seeing women in clinging satin nightgowns or short lacy teddies. No doubt his private life was other than monastic, and she felt a foolish pang of feminine jealousy. He must be used to women clients calling him at night for reassurance.

''Gail?'' He broke the weighted silence.

She cleared her throat. ''Thanks for taking the time to talk with me. Now I think I'd better get some rest.''

''Are you sure you don't want me to come over? I'm a good watchdog.''

''No, thanks.''

''Positive?''

''Yes,'' she lied.

''Then I'll see you tomorrow. I have a couple of meetings, but how about a cup of coffee in the cafeteria tomorrow after your therapy session?''

She readily agreed.

"Till tomorrow then."

"Tomorrow."

They told each other good-night three times before they finally hung up.

CURTIS CALLED LAMONT the next morning. The report from officers Kline and Mantelli had already crossed the detective's desk. "Apparently, the search of the house was negative. Maybe Miss Richards was having a case of jitters. That's the way it is when someone feels threatened. They see danger behind every bush."

"Gail isn't like that!" Curtis snapped. "If she said she heard something, it wasn't her imagination. You know she's not the kind to have hysterics."

The detective ignored the challenge. "Something else came across my desk. A widow, Mrs. Jasper Wilhite, made a report that I found very interesting. It seems she brought in a couple of interesting packages and notes that she'd found while getting her house ready for sale."

"Packages? Not the same kind...?"

"Exactly. A bloody child's dress and a mutilated doll, complete with ugly nursery rhymes. They had her husband's name on them."

Curtis's mouth suddenly felt dry. "You said she was a widow. What happened to Mr. Wilhite?"

"He committed suicide. Found asphyxiated in his garage. The Wilhites were separated at the time and so she didn't know about the harassment until she found the ugly things when cleaning out a small greenhouse they had in the back. Apparently the marriage had gone on the rocks shortly after Jasper Wilhite was involved in an automobile accident that killed their little girl.''

The parallels were unmistakable, thought Curtis. Sherrie Sinclair, Jasper Wilhite and Gail. All three involved in accidents, all three the target of someone carrying out a vendetta.

''Sounds familiar, doesn't it?'' Then Lamont swore. ''Too damn familiar.''

Curtis had to ask the question even though he wasn't certain he was ready to hear the answer. ''Is there a possibility that Sherrie and Wilhite didn't commit suicide?''

Lamont didn't hesitate. ''A very big one.''

After Curtis hung up, the name Jasper Wilhite kept tugging at his memory. He was certain the man had never been a client of his, but he could have been a patient at Crestview.

''Myra, would you see if the main computer has anything on Jasper Wilhite?'' he asked his secretary.

Myra was wearing a new wine-colored suit and a silk blouse that was flattering to her auburn hair and tanned skin. Irritation flickered over her face when Curtis didn't even look up. He stared preoccupied at some papers in front of him.

''Was he a rehab client?''

Curtis forced a patient smile. ''That's what I want to find out. I don't remember the name but he could have been an outpatient from another division.''

Myra raised a well-plucked eyebrow. ''What's up?''

Usually he appreciated his secretary's interest in the various cases, but he wasn't about to clue her in on

Gail Richards's harassment. The rumor mill at Crestview was well oiled and he knew that Gail could easily become the object of morbid curiosity. "Check on it, will you?" His tone was a little sharp.

She had the information for him in less than fifteen minutes. Curtis found that his hands were slightly sweaty as he read the report. Jasper Wilhite had never been a Colorado rehabilitation client, but he had been sent to Crestview by his doctor for an evaluation and had been an outpatient for about ten days. Curtis decided he must have heard the man's name at that time.

A notation had been made about his problem with alcohol and a pending divorce. Those factors, plus the death of their child in a car accident were certainly enough to drive an unstable man to suicide, thought Curtis. The fact that the man had briefly been an outpatient at Crestview didn't clarify anything. A lot of accident victims were referred to the center.

"Did you find out what you wanted to know?" asked Myra, and Curtis realized she had been watching him all the time she'd pretended to file some folders in a nearby cabinet. "Are we going to get him as a client?"

"No, he's deceased."

Myra closed the drawer very slowly and turned around. "Then why...?" The question dangled in the air half finished.

Curtis reached for a pile of papers and handed them to her. "These are ready to be entered."

She opened her mouth to say something, then closed it. Her eyes narrowed as she gave him a searching look. Then, with an impatient shrug, she turned and left.

Curtis knew his secretary wouldn't let go. Myra would make more inquiries and shortly everyone at Crestview would know that the rehab office was interested in Jasper Wilhite. Curtis had the feeling that he unwittingly started some kind of a dangerous domino action.

GAIL EXPERIENCED a flash of disappointment when she entered the cafeteria after her exercise session and failed to see Curtis at any of the small tables. A few people were scattered about the room, mostly staff in white uniforms on their afternoon breaks.

She sat down at a table where she could see the door. The decor was pleasant with gaily painted walls in shades of blue and planters filled with green foliage. What if he didn't come? Already a sense of loneliness was stealing over her as she listened to the laughter and chatter coming from the other tables. Maybe some other client had required his time and attention. He had told her he had nearly a hundred clients in his program. She ordered herself to be reasonable. Undoubtedly, demands were made on his time by other people who probably wanted the same kind of personal attention. She had no right to expect him to drop everything. She jumped.

"It's just me," said Curtis, coming up behind her with two cups of coffee in his hands. "I went through the line. Didn't know if you took cream, but brought a couple, anyway."

She shook her head. "Black."

"Me too." He gave her that special smile that somehow made them kindred spirits. "How did the therapy go?"

"Not well, I'm afraid." She held her cup with both hands to keep it from shaking.

"It's no wonder. You've been marvelous to function at all after the last couple of days." He reached out and touched her hand. "I'm there for you. You know that, don't you?"

She nodded.

He gave her a smile that didn't erase the worried creases in his forehead. She had begun to read his body language. He was uptight about something.

"What is it? Have you heard from Lieutenant Lamont?" A nervous fluttering tightened her stomach muscles.

Curtis took a sip of coffee before replying. She knew from the way the muscles in his cheeks tensed that he was trying to reach a decision. Finally, he said, "I wouldn't be telling you this if I didn't think you had a right to know... and could handle it."

"Try me," she said, keeping a steady gaze on his face.

"You and Sherrie aren't the only ones to be on the receiving end of nursery rhyme threats and macabre packages. We know of at least one more... a Jasper Wilhite. He was here at Crestview for a few weeks after a car accident in which his little girl was killed. He was driving under the influence."

Gail's eyes widened. "You've talked to him?"

"Unfortunately, no. He's dead. Committed suicide—asphyxiated in his garage. I guess he couldn't face the future. His marriage was on the rocks, he was filled with guilt over the loss of his child, had a drinking problem—so he killed himself."

"No, he didn't!" piped up a squeaky voice. "That's a lie."

At first they couldn't tell where the voice was coming from. No one was sitting at any of the tables near them. A slight movement lowered their eyes and the mystery was solved. Scuffy sat Indian-style under a table just behind them, her crutches parked against a nearby wall. The little girl was half hidden by one of the planters, but she leaned around it, peering up with round eyes at Gail and Curtis.

"You blasted little eavesdropper," swore Curtis. "Don't you know you could get your bottom warmed for snooping on people?"

She pursed her little mouth. Her carrot hair stuck out around her head like a kinky broom. She reminded Gail of a mischievous monkey.

"Come out of there." He reached for her.

Gail couldn't help but choke back a chuckle as Curtis retrieved the child from under the table and sat her down in a chair between them. The brazen little girl wasn't the least bit cowed by Curtis's lecture.

"Well, he didn't!" she countered, ignoring the scolding as Curtis paused for breath.

Gail leaned forward. "What do you mean, Scuffy?"

"That man didn't kill himself. He didn't asph... asph...whatever you said."

Gail exchanged a quick look with Curtis. "How do you know, Scuffy?" she asked evenly.

"'Cause he promised to give me some stamps for my collection."

"You knew Jasper Wilhite?" demanded Curtis.

"He was here...wasn't he? And he was nice to me...not like some of the dorks around this place. I used to sneak down to his room all the time. He gave me candy." Her pugnacious chin came out. "And when he left he promised to send me some stamps for my book."

Such is the faith of children, thought Gail sadly.

"I'm sure he meant to keep the promise, Scuffy," said Curtis solemnly. "But after Mr. Wilhite went home...some things happened to him...and he became very sad and decided he didn't want to go on living."

"No!" she yelled into Curtis's face, clenching her little fist. "That's not true. He was going on a trip to Mexico—he told me so. And he promised that he would bring me back some stamps."

Gail and Curtis exchanged glances—what kind of tale was this?

"When?" asked Curtis patiently. "When did he tell you that?"

Scuffy hesitated. "Well, he didn't exactly *tell* me."

"Then how did you know he was planning a trip to Mexico?" he prodded.

"'Cause he sent me a note. I got it the day before they say he died." Scuffy turned her brown saucer eyes on Gail. "He gave me a pretty red book...with a whole bunch of stamps in it."

"That's nice."

"Could I see the note, Scuffy?" asked Curtis. "Do you still have it?"

She shook her tousled head. "Naw, I lost it. But I have the stamp album. Want to see that?"

Curtis exchanged skeptical glances with Gail.

"You don't believe me, do you?" The little girl's eyes snapped. "Nobody does. But I know lots of things."

"Probably more than what's good for you," conceded Curtis with a wry smile.

Just then a pretty brunette nurse, Ellyn McPherson, came in the cafeteria and a look of relief crossed her face when she saw Scuffy. "There you are. The floor supervisor is having a fit."

She looked at Curtis and blushed. "Sorry to interrupt." Then she lowered her long eyelashes before peering at him. "I haven't seen you around much lately. You don't have lunch at the same time you used to. I asked Myra and she said you usually had a sandwich at your desk"

"A workaholic, that's me," said Curtis smoothly. Ellyn glanced at Gail in a speculative way, but Curtis didn't follow through with an introduction. "We'll talk later, Scuffy," he said, handing her the crutches.

Ellyn gave Curtis a smile that was over and above anything the situation called for as she led Scuffy out of the cafeteria.

"She's very pretty," said Gail in a conversational tone.

"And very young," said Curtis in a tone that put an end to that topic of conversation.

Gail felt foolishly relieved. "What do you think? Is the child telling the truth?"

Curtis took a sip of coffee before answering. "I honestly don't know. Scuffy is a consummate liar. And knows how to manipulate people. When she heard us talking about Wilhite, she could have made the whole thing up." He was silent for a moment and then he added quietly, "But I don't think that a man contemplating suicide would be in the frame of mind to write a note to a little girl, promising her postage stamps."

Chapter Ten

Gail went to bed early that night and enjoyed a deep, dreamless sleep. She awakened in the morning with a surge of new vitality that surprised her. *I'm getting better.* The knowledge put a glow on the morning and her good spirits were not even diminished by Inga's usual glower as the housekeeper set a bowl of cold cereal and a piece of scraped toast on the table in front of Gail. There was a pugnacious jut to her broad chin as if she expected an argument.

Gail just smiled and said, "Thank you, Inga." She wasn't going to let the sour-faced young woman dim her high spirits. The morning got even better when Curtis stopped by the house on his way to the office.

Gail greeted him with clear, sparkling eyes and a lilt in her voice. "You're just in time to join me for a second cup of coffee."

He told himself that he was just tending to business as he carried two cups into her sitting room. "Everything is set for Scuffy to begin her lessons," he said. "I have the authorization for three tutoring sessions a week. Someone from the center will bring her over.

She may be less than cooperative. And I warn you, she has sticky fingers."

"Scuffy steals?"

He nodded. "I checked out that story of the stamp album. It disappeared from Jasper Wilhite's room and the cleaning lady found it hidden in Scuffy's things. They made her return it, but Wilhite decided to let her have the album. He seems to have had a soft spot for the kid, but I'm afraid all that business about him promising her stamps is another wild tale. Scuffy claims she lost the note, but nobody at Crestview remembers anything about it. You have to give the kid credit for creativity." He smiled wryly. "Very little gets past her freckled pug nose."

"I'm sure we'll get along fine. Most of our students are something of a challenge."

They talked a few more minutes about testing and establishing some realistic goals for bringing Scuffy's reading up to grade level. Curtis was impressed with Gail's command of reading approaches and materials. No wonder she was reaching such a wide range of learning disabilities. Her enthusiasm was infectious, and he loved the way her eyes shined as she talked. Reluctantly he looked at his watch. Myra would be having a fit.

He stood up to go. "There's a little party tonight...for one of my clients who's going home from Crestview," he told Gail. "Just a small gathering in the cafeteria. I was wondering...if you feel up to it...maybe you'd like to join us. I promise to bring you home the minute you get tired."

Gail searched his expression and then smiled, satisfied. "I'd love to go," she said.

"Good. I'll pick you up at eight."

When Gail came home from therapy that afternoon, she took a long warm bath, curled her hair and did her nails. She was ready and waiting when he arrived, feeling foolishly like a young girl on her first date. She had examined her wardrobe for the right thing to wear, and the way his eyes smiled as they traveled over her pink angora sweater and matching tight-fitting stirrup pants, she knew she had chosen right. She hoped the dainty turquoise necklace with matching earrings reflected the same shade of her own eyes.

Curtis wore a colorful harlequin sweater and casual full slacks that would make him the focal point in any ski lodge, she thought as she pictured him flushed and tanned from a day on the slopes.

THE SMALL CAFETERIA at the center was festive with balloons and a Good Luck cake set in the middle of a long table. The honored guest was a young girl in her teens who had broken both legs in a skiing accident. With the resiliency of youth she had mended so beautifully that only a slight limp remained. She laughed with good humor as she opened gag gifts like a tennis racket without strings and a bedpan covered with heart-shaped decals. Larry gave her a giant Band-Aid a foot long, and Gail could tell from the way the girl blushed that the personable orderly had made another conquest.

Gail sat with Curtis at an inconspicuous table where they could be a part of the activities but safely out of the boisterous bustle. Curtis was perfectly at ease, but Gail was a little uncomfortable. She was conscious of pointed looks in their direction and open speculation about their being there together.

There had been an unpleasant moment soon after their arrival when his attractive secretary had stopped by the table. Myra put her hands lightly on his shoulders, bent over and whispered rather loudly, "Putting in overtime?"

A glint of anger flashed in Curtis's eyes as he answered, "Strictly pleasure."

Myra wore a short green wool dress with matching suede boots. Her measuring glance went over Gail's fair hair, freed from her usual French braid and drifting nicely around her face in soft curls. Gail's soft pink outfit made Myra's bold green ensemble seem rather tawdry. Something icy glinted in her large blue eyes. "So nice you could come to our little party, Miss Richards."

"I appreciate Curtis inviting me."

"He really puts himself out for his clients, doesn't he? They all love Curtis dearly. No wonder he has more successful closures than anyone."

"Myra—"

She dismissed his warning tone with a wave of her hand. "It's true and you know it, Curtis, dear. Not many counselors would extend their working day into the evening just to help their clients adjust. You're very fortunate, Miss Richards."

"Gail's company is no sacrifice, Myra," Curtis countered shortly.

She gave him a knowing smile and moved away.

Gail's spirits plunged. She had only come with Curtis because she had decided the invitation was a personal one, not a professional obligation. For the first time in years, she wanted to let the barriers down, allow herself to become interested in an attractive man. Myra's remarks made Gail realize how much she resented the idea that Curtis's attention might merely be a "duty." Was he just looking out for her welfare as he would any of his clients? Had she let her emotions blind her?

Curtis reached over and took her hand firmly in his. As he lightly stroked the softest of her flesh his touch sent warmth spiraling. At that moment Roberta Benson stopped at their table with a coffeepot in her hand.

"Refill?" Dressed in a black-and-white jumpsuit that complemented her dark hair, and wearing pearl earrings, she looked less like a girls' gym teacher. She eyed Gail as she filled their cups. "Glad to see I didn't wear you out today, Miss Richards. I thought we had a pretty good session this afternoon."

Gail was tempted to confess that by the time the therapist had finished with her, she thought she would never move again. Instead, she lied and said she felt good after the workout.

Roberta just smiled, and Gail wondered if the therapist was thinking that maybe she'd been too easy. "See you tomorrow," Roberta said with a promise in her tone. As she moved on, Gail mentally groaned, wondering if she'd set herself up for an accelerated grueling pace the next session.

Beth Scott came around, passing a plate of cookies. The look she sent Gail was both apprehensive and defensive. Gail felt Beth was just waiting for her to cause trouble about the tank accident and was ready to lash out in order to protect her job. When Curtis teased her about the cookies, Beth's expression eased.

"My grandmother's recipe . . . took a prize at the Texas State Fair," Beth bragged. "Best ginger cookies you'll ever taste."

She waited until Curtis munched one and nodded in agreement. "Good . . . good."

Satisfied, Beth took the platter to the next table. When her back was turned, Curtis secreted the remaining half of the cookie in a napkin and took a drink of water to ease the biting ginger taste.

Gail laughed and offered him the two cookies that Beth had pressed on her.

"No, thanks. I think Beth misread dear old grandmother's recipe. Too much ginger. I suspect she doesn't know the difference between a teaspoon and tablespoon."

By this time several couples had begun dancing to some records. Tables had been pushed back to form a small dance floor. Gail noticed that Larry changed partners with each dance. Once he looked over in Gail's direction and called "Want to dance, Miss Richards?"

She laughed and shook her head. Curtis put his arm across the back of Gail's chair in a protective gesture and called back. "Down, Romeo."

Larry laughed and pulled a pretty brunette nurse to her feet and they began gyrating around each other.

"They're very good. Is that the nurse who came after Scuffy yesterday?" asked Gail.

He nodded. "Ellyn McPherson. Nice girl." A worried frown crossed his face. "She's way out of her league with Larry."

Gail was aware that more than one woman looked in Curtis's direction with a hopeful glance. She tried to get him to dance with someone else. When he shook his head, she asked, "Don't you like to dance?"

"Not that modern stuff. Give me a wailing saxophone, soft lights and lovely Gail Richards floating in my arms. Now that's worth waiting for."

When his eyes locked with hers, her stomach quivered as if she were sliding down a rainbow. She was embarrassed by the warmth she felt flooding in her face. In order to get her emotions under control, she excused herself and walked down the hall to the ladies' rest room.

While she was there, Ellyn came in but didn't acknowledge Gail's presence as they stood together at the long mirror. The pretty girl gave a quick flip to her hair, moistened her lips and then darted out again. Gail smiled to herself. She remembered those breathless moments of youth. Looking at her own reflection, she saw a sparkle in her own eyes. She laughed, moistened her lips and gave a pat to her own hair.

As she came out of the rest room, she caught a glimpse of Larry's back as he disappeared through the outside door at the end of the corridor. She wondered which woman was his conquest for the night. Ellyn? Curtis wouldn't be happy about that.

A gray-haired nurse hurrying down the hall stopped Gail. "Have you seen a small girl with red hair?"

"Scuffy?"

"Oh, you know her? She's supposed to be in her room, but I can't find her anywhere. I thought that maybe she'd sneaked down to the party."

Gail smothered a smile. "Well, I haven't seen her...but I haven't been looking under all the tables, either."

"I declare I don't know what to do...short of handcuffing her to the bed. The minute you turn your back she's gone."

"I imagine that life gets boring for a little girl her age," said Gail in Scuffy's defense. "I understand she's been in and out of hospitals all her life."

"Well, it's my guess she's been expelled from half of them," declared the exasperated nurse.

When Gail returned to the table, she told Curtis about Scuffy's disappearing act. They both laughed and decided it would serve the little truant right if she stole some of Beth's cookies.

The party was still humming when Gail pleaded fatigue and Curtis quickly secured her wrap. They paused to congratulate the young girl on her going-home party and the way she hugged Curtis, Gail knew that he had been important in her recovery. No question about it, he was good at his job.

Snow had fallen while they were at the party, turning the parking lot white. Curtis offered to bring the car around to the door, but Gail refused. She slipped her arm through his. "If you'll hold on to me, I'll be fine."

"My pleasure." He deliberately tightened his grip until his body brushed hers with every step. Layers of cloth did nothing to lessen the intimate contact between them as they moved side by side across the parking lot.

The night was luminous with reflected light. A pristine whiteness covered cars and trees and a smooth carpet of snow spread over the grounds. The new snow was undisturbed except for one set of car tracks and the footprints Gail and Curtis left behind them as they walked toward his car.

The moment was a lovely one—until Curtis stiffened, stopped and held her back.

"What?" She blinked snowflakes off her eyelashes, straining to see what he was staring at. If he hadn't been holding on tightly to her, her knees might have given.

Lying directly in front of them was a crumpled body with snowy car tracks going right over it.

Chapter Eleven

"Can you stand here just a minute...while I have a look?"

Gail nodded and braced herself with her cane. She watched Curtis kneel down by the prone figure and feel for a pulse. She couldn't tell if it was a man or woman lying there half covered with snow. There wasn't any movement, and after a moment Curtis shook his head.

He came back to her. "Come on, I'll get you in the car and then I'll go back and call the police."

The wind quickened at that moment and sent snow whipping across the open area like a miniblizzard. Curtis sheltered Gail as much as possible as he guided her to the car. He wrapped a car blanket around her legs and started the engine. "It'll be warm in a minute." He searched her face anxiously. "You'll be all right?"

"Fine...I'll be fine. Don't worry." She hoped her voice didn't betray the tremors in the pit of her stomach. "What do you think happened?"

"Looks like a hit-and-run. I'll take care of things and then drive you home."

"Did you recognize ... ?"

He paused for a moment, braced in the open door against the wind and flying snow. Then he nodded. "Larry. He's dead."

He shut the door, and Gail sat there in a numbed shock. Her mind refused to function. Denial was the only mental state she allowed herself. There had been some mistake. Larry wasn't dead. He was laughing, joking and flirting with some girl. Nobody was more alive than Larry. He couldn't be lying motionless in the snow.

Gail was vaguely aware of voices and the arrival of a police car. Then the piercing squeal and the flashing lights of an ambulance filled the parking lot with frantic activity. As she sat in the cocoon of the car, she was strangely isolated from the tragedy that her mind refused to accept.

When Curtis came back to the car, he looked grim. "I'll take you home now," he said. His glance was anxious as it passed over her rigid profile.

They didn't speak until they arrived at her house. He turned off the engine and reached for her. At first she remained rigid in his embrace, but he laid his head against hers, not saying anything, just holding her. Slowly, like someone recovering from a chill, she shuddered and relaxed against him. She felt strangely renewed, healed by a passionate desire between them. For the moment, the world and all its ugliness faded away.

He kissed her then, working her lips gently against his until warmth sped through her and life poured back into her body. His fingers flexed lightly upon her cheeks as he tenderly held her face in his hands. His kisses parted her lips, and his flicking tongue teased her until a soft moan escaped from her throat. Radiating heat rose deep within her and mocked snow crystals whipping against the windows of the car.

"I better take you in," he murmured, burying his lips in the warm curve of her neck. She threaded her fingers through moist dark hair falling on his forehead and then winced as she shifted toward him.

He pulled back instantly. "Forgive me, I . . ."

"No, it's all right," she assured him. "I'm not . . . fragile."

"Well, I don't think this is the place to prove your point." He kissed the tip of her nose. "I think a nice cold walk to the house is in order."

He had parked in the driveway, so they mounted the steps on the end of the porch. As they walked to the front door, he kept his arm tightly around her and she gave in to the impulse to lay her head back against his shoulder. She had left a light on in the hall and her sitting room. Once they were inside, his hands lingered on her shoulders as he helped her off with her coat.

"Would you like . . ." she began.

A demanding ring of the library phone vibrated through the hall.

"I'll get it," said Curtis.

By the time Gail entered the library, he was protesting vigorously. "No. I told you everything there is to know. Miss Richards can't add anything more. No need to drag her into it." He glared as he listened and then snapped, "But that's absurd. She hardly knew him. Larry was an orderly at Crestview...Gail is a patient at Crestview...and that's the only connection. Give the woman a break, for heaven's sake!" There was a lengthy pause. "I've told you exactly how we found the body. I assure you she has nothing to add to your report." With a crisp goodbye, he hung up.

While he had been talking, Gail had eased down into a chair, her chest suddenly tight as she watched anger sweep up into his face. All euphoria had dissipated. Cold reality was back. She moistened her dry lips. "Who was it?"

Curtis muttered a couple of swearwords. "The officer checking out the accident. I don't know whether I got him off your neck or not. Bad luck that we were the first ones to stumble on the body. I told him you have nothing to add, but he'll be over tomorrow. It seems that—" He hesitated.

"What is it?"

With a dismissive wave of his hand Curtis said, "It's really stupid. Apparently he's been talking to people at the party. Someone told him that Larry left the cafeteria about the same time you did...you know, when you went to the ladies' room. Apparently no one saw him after that."

Curtis watched the color fade from Gail's face. "What happened? Was Larry following you?"

"Of course not. It's just that I saw Larry...I mean, I caught a glimpse of him leaving the building when I was in the hall."

"Was he alone?"

"I don't think so." She frowned. "I had the impression that someone was with him, but I could have been just jumping to conclusions. Knowing Larry, I assumed that he had some girl in tow." She subdued rising nausea. "He must have been run over shortly after that."

Curtis solemnly agreed. "We didn't stay long after you came back."

"How could it have happened?" Gail's voice was strained.

"He could have been hit by some driver who was blinded by the snow," Curtis speculated. "Or maybe someone was pulling out of the lot and didn't have the windshield cleared enough to see."

"Surely the driver would have known he'd hit someone," protested Gail. "How could anyone just drive off and . . . and leave Larry there?"

"That's the way with hit-and-run accidents," Curtis said angrily. "Larry must have been knocked down and then the car wheel went right over him."

Gail shuddered. "I hope he died instantly. I hate to think of him lying there . . . like that."

"If it wasn't hit-and-run?" Curtis questioned solemnly.

"What else could it be?" Her eyes rounded.

"It's possible that Larry could have been dead before the car drove over him," he said quietly.

"What?" She stared at him in disbelief. "You're saying it was deliberate?"

"I'm just speculating," he responded in a reasonable tone.

"But that's absurd. If there's anyone that everybody liked, it was Larry." She put a hand to the back of her neck where a headache was beginning to throb.

"Why would anyone want to harm a nice guy like that?"

"Doesn't seem likely, does it. Sorry I brought it up. I better go and let you get some rest. I'm driving to Colorado Springs early in the morning. I have an all-day conference and dinner meeting. Probably won't get back until late." He bent over her chair and asked softly, "Will you be all right?"

For an answer, she lifted her face to his and he gave her a lingering kiss that left them both breathing heavily. Emotion made her voice husky as she said his name. "Curtis?"

He waited.

She gave him a weak smile and then took a deep breath. "Good night, Mr. O'Mallory." Her voice was strangely husky.

A smile curved the corner of his lips. "Good night, Miss Richards. Sleep well, pretty lady. I'll call you tomorrow night when I get back. Try to put the accident out of your mind."

"The whole thing is so awful...."

"I know. But it doesn't have anything to do with you," he said firmly and kissed her again.

"It doesn't have anything to do with you." Gail clung to his reassurance after he'd gone, and she lay stiffly in bed waiting for her medicine to ease the pain in her back and head. On the edge of sleep, she wondered why she had been afraid to trust her own feelings. Would Curtis have stayed the night if she'd had the courage to ask him?

GAIL STILL HAD the headache in the morning when she awakened to Inga's heavy steps and the banging of pots and pans. Gail dreaded facing the woman's hostile personality, and she vowed to call the employment agency and see if Mrs. Rosales was ready to return to work.

By the time Gail had dressed and made her way to the kitchen, she could smell coffee and the odor of warm pastry. She found the housekeeper was sitting at the table reading the morning paper. Inga lowered the page and peered at Gail with curiosity glinting in her blue eyes.

"You got your name in the paper." Satisfied with Gail's startled look, she started reading as if she were delivering tasty morsels with every word. The account was brief, stating that Larry Smith, an orderly at Crestview Rehabilitation Center, had been run over in the parking lot at approximately eleven o'clock. Inga's voice rose as she continued, "His body was found by Mr. Curtis O'Mallory and Miss Gail Richards as they left a farewell party given at the center's cafeteria. The police—"

"A cup of coffee, please, Inga," Gail cut in briskly as she sat down in her usual kitchen chair.

Inga laid the paper down with a shrug and stood up. "I guess you don't need to read about something you saw with your own eyes. Must have been pretty upsetting, though. Finding some guy dead in the road." She looked down at Gail. "No wonder you look awful this morning. You're taking too much of that painkiller stuff, if you ask me."

Nobody asked you. "Coffee, please?"

Inga's eyebrows knitted together as she turned away. Gail picked up the paper, straightened it out and turned to her favorite columnist. She read a few lines, but the pain behind her eyes wouldn't let her focus on the print. She put it down and was sipping her coffee and pecking at a blueberry muffin when the doorbell rang.

Inga impatiently flung down the dish towel and left the kitchen to answer it. A moment later she came back and informed Gail that a Lieutenant Lamont was waiting for her in the sitting room.

Gail was tempted to tell Inga to notify the detective that she was spending the day in bed and couldn't see anyone, but her housekeeper's hawklike eyes mocked such weakness. Why did she have the feeling that Inga was enjoying every minute of her distress?

Lieutenant Lamont was instantly apologetic as Gail came into the room. "Sorry, Miss Richards, to be calling so early in the morning." His sharp eyes seemed to take in the deep shadows in her cheeks and pained lines in her forehead. "I didn't get you up, did I?"

"No, I was just finishing breakfast. Please sit down, Lieutenant. Would you like a cup of coffee?" she asked politely.

"No, thanks. I just had one."

He waited until she was seated before saying, "I'll just take a few minutes of your time."

Was he here to question her about Larry? Gail stifled a spurt of impatience. It was bad enough to have her name in the newspaper as having found the victim. Now she was going to be grilled for knowledge that she didn't have. She was surprised when he started talking about Scuffy—not Larry.

"I talked to the little girl at the rehab center. Curtis told me what she'd said about receiving a written message from Jasper Wilhite the day before he killed himself. I thought I'd better check it out. What was your impression, Miss Richards? You must know kids pretty well. Do you think she'd be telling the truth?"

"I've only talked with the child a couple of times," replied Gail. "She has a reputation for getting into trouble, and she obviously gives the staff headaches." Gail paused. "Sometimes it's difficult to tell when she's telling the truth and when she's making up a good story. Anyway, she told us Mr. Wilhite had given her the album and had promised to send her some stamps."

"From Mexico?"

Gail nodded. "When Curtis asked to see the note she said Wilhite had sent her, Scuffy said she'd lost it."

Lamont nodded. "That's what she told me, too. So we only have her word for it. Did you think it's likely she made the whole thing up... on the spot?"

Gail thought back to the way Scuffy had interrupted their conversation, yelling out "No" when Curtis had said that Wilhite had killed himself. Scuffy's eyes had snapped and there had been an intense expression on her little face. Gail sensed a lot of emotion behind her protest. "I don't think she made up the story on the spot," said Gail slowly.

"Then you believe she was telling the truth?"

"About the note? I don't know...but I'm pretty sure Scuffy didn't just make up the story for Curtis's and my benefit."

Lamont shoved his glasses back in an impatient gesture. "Well, I didn't get anywhere with her. I understand she's coming here to be tutored in reading."

"She's scheduled for one o'clock...with my substitute teacher." Gail didn't tell him she had reservations about Miss Crum's being able to handle the little girl. She had the feeling the woman would be putty in Scuffy's hands.

"Is there any chance you could talk with the child...maybe get a little more specifics about the alleged note from Wilhite?"

"Is it important?"

"It could be. A man who writes a little girl one day that he's going to bring her back some stamps from a trip he's planning, and then asphyxiates himself in his garage the next must have had a change of heart or..." The lieutenant left the rest of the sentence dangling.

Gail didn't have any difficulty finishing it. *Or he didn't kill himself.*

SCUFFY ARRIVED a little before one o'clock. Gail didn't see who brought her but the little girl announced, "I'm supposed to go back with you in the Ambu-Cab."

Good, thought Gail. That would give them a chance to get better acquainted. She introduced Scuffy to Miss Crum, and the substitute teacher bobbed around Scuffy like a mother hen with a new chick. Scuffy's bright eyes took in everything in the room and then she pointed to a computer that had a color monitor. "I want to play on that!"

Miss Crum gave a merry laugh. "Let's read in this nice little book...."

"No!" She stuck out her chin. "I hate books."

"Now, sweetheart," cooed Miss Crum. "Be a little angel and read this nice story for me. Then we'll play a little game with these letters."

"No! I hate games."

Gail bit her lip to keep from interfering. She sent a silent message to Angie. Many obstreperous kids had met their match when her assistant took over. If anyone could get Scuffy under control, Angie could, thought Gail, as she made a quiet exit from the room.

When it was time for the Ambu-Cab, Angie brought Scuffy into the sitting room. She sent Gail an exasperated look that told her that Scuffy's first day at the Learning House had not gone well.

On the way to Crestview in the Ambu-Cab, Gail asked Scuffy how the lesson went.

The little girl leveled accusing eyes at Gail. "You were supposed to learn me to read."

"Teach you to read," Gail corrected.

"Yeah. I'm going to tell Mr. O'Mallory I ain't going over there to play games." Her chin quivered. "I ain't no dummy."

"Of course you're not. And you'll learn to read. I promise you." Gail knew that playing games and reading "baby" books made any student believe himself to be a failure. She'd seen the same anxiety in young and old—Keith, who was dyslexic, Mr. Devitto whose native tongue wasn't English and children like Scuffy who had been tossed about in an educational mixer. All of them were faced with an uphill battle to master the mystery of written symbols.

According to Angie, Edith Crum had refused to follow the usual curriculum and testing program for new students.

"I'll work with you myself," Gail promised on an optimistic note. Somehow she would manage her energy to make good on the promise. Remembering Lamont's request, she said casually, "I'd really like to see your stamp album."

Scuffy's brown eyes measured her with childish frankness. "Why?"

"Because I've never seen a *real* stamp album."

Scuffy never blinked. "I'll bring it next time."

Gail smiled. "Good. And I'd like to see the note Mr. Wilhite sent you, if you find it."

The little girl set her pugnacious chin. "You're just like all the rest. You're trying to trick me."

"I just want you to tell the truth. Did you get a note from Mr. Wilhite?"

Scuffy's eyes suddenly filled with tears. "He was my friend."

Gail put her arm around the little girl. "And I bet he liked you a lot, too."

Scuffy swiped at her eyes with her sleeve. Gail handed her a tissue and kept her arm around her shoulder all the way to the center. "You can work on the computer next time," she promised.

Ellyn McPherson met the Ambu-Cab, and her pretty face was drawn and pale. Gail remembered the way she and Larry had danced together, moving gracefully in suggestive motions and laughing at each other with shining eyes. As Ellyn pushed Gail's wheelchair down the familiar hall, she sniffed. "I can't believe it."

"Neither can I," admitted Gail. She remembered how grateful she'd been for his friendly welcome. He'd always greeted her with a cocky grin, teased and flattered her. No matter how nervous or tired she'd been, he'd been able to make her smile.

Everyone at the center was in a somber mood. Beth didn't have two words to say, and Roberta went through Gail's exercises in a mechanical fashion. Several of the young nurses had red eyes from crying.

A gray-haired policeman asked to speak with Gail when she was finished with her therapy session. His questions centered on Gail's trip to the ladies' rest room at the same time Larry left the dance floor. She told him that she had glimpsed Larry going out the side door but was not certain whether he had been alone.

He thanked her for her cooperation, but Gail had the feeling that he was convinced that she was holding back something. Gail was glad when it was time to go home. She walked to the Ambu-Cab without her cane—the only bright note in a dismal day.

When she got back to the house, she found a note from Angie saying that two more students had canceled their scheduled lessons—said they weren't coming back until Gail was able to teach them. Since they were the only students scheduled, Angie and Edith Crum had decided to call it a day.

Gail expected to find Inga in the kitchen but there was no sign of her... nor sign of dinner preparation, either. Wearily, Gail walked down the hall to her bedroom, taking cautious steps because her leg muscles were tired and a headache was gathering momentum behind her temples. Intent on getting a couple of aspirin, she started into the bathroom.

"Wh—?" She stopped, stunned by what she saw.

Inga stood in front of the mirror. The young woman's face was grotesque with heavy mascara and deep brown eye shadow turning her eyes into dark sockets. Bloodred lipstick made her mouth look as if it had been sliced with a razor. Her hair had been teased until it stood out wildly all over her head. Gail's cosmetic bag was open and the contents spread all over the sink.

For a moment Inga didn't move. As she met Gail's stunned expression in the mirror, she didn't say anything—and neither did her eyes. Slowly she put down an eyebrow pencil and began putting all of the things back in the cosmetic bag. Then she wet a washrag and began wiping her face.

Gail watched her for a long moment before she found her voice. "Please leave, Inga...and don't come back." Gail turned and went into her bedroom and shut the door.

Gail stood leaning against the door, praying that Inga wouldn't thrust it open and angrily confront her. The lock was an old-fashioned one that took a skeleton key—the kind she didn't have.

She waited. Her heartbeat was a loud drumming in her. It seemed forever before she heard Inga's heavy steps going down the hall and the back door of the house slammed shut.

Gail waited a few more minutes before she allowed herself to cautiously open the door and peek out. The bathroom was empty and her cosmetics were back in their proper place.

"Thank God." She sat down heavily on the bed. Her headache had grown into a crescendo of pain. She swallowed a pill from her medicine bottle. Then she stretched out on the bed. Her clock said four-thirty. She'd rest for an hour and then open a can of soup for supper.

An exhausted sleep claimed her and a nighttime sky showed through the high bedroom window when she was wakened by an odious stench. She sat up and for a moment thought she was going to retch. The foul odor turned her stomach and brought bile up into her mouth. She cupped her nose with one hand and turned on her bed light with the other. Her frantic gaze swept the room and saw nothing responsible for the vile smell.

It must be coming from the kitchen. Swallowing repeatedly to control the churning in her stomach, she made her way down the hall. The odious smell increased with each step. When she reached the kitchen doorway, she surveyed the room, trying to locate the cause of the disgusting stench.

The room was clean and orderly. With eyes smarting, she walked across the kitchen to the back porch. When she reached the doorway, she gasped with disbelief.

Rotten broken eggs were everywhere, splattered on the walls and windows, and soiling the things she had stored there. The sulfuric stench was overpowering, but what sent her to gagging were bloody chicken feathers and entrails strewed across the floor to the outside door.

Chapter Twelve

Lieutenant Lamont was not at the police station when Gail called from the library phone. "Is there a message, ma'am?"

Gail fought a wave of hysteria. No message could convey the despair she felt at having someone defile her home in such an unspeakable way.

"Perhaps you could speak to someone else?" suggested the dispatcher in the weighty silence.

How could she explain the situation to someone else? She couldn't bring herself to go into all the details of the previous harassments. She firmed her voice. "No, I'll wait for the lieutenant. Tell him that Miss Richards's home has been vandalized again. He'll understand."

"Yes, Miss Richards. I'll tell the lieutenant as soon as he checks in."

"Do you know when that might be?" Her voice cracked. Even though she had shut the door to the porch, the vile stench had already invaded the front part of the house. Every breath she drew was a reminder of the bloody chicken parts and malodorous eggs.

"It shouldn't be more than an hour or two," the dispatcher assured her.

An hour or two? *An eternity.* Gail hung up and sat motionless in front of the phone. Several times she reached for it and then pulled back. No. She'd always been able to handle her own problems. Even when she lay helpless in the hospital, she had drawn on her own resources and she'd always been critical of others who couldn't go it alone. Now she found herself teetering on the edge of pure panic. These vile acts against her had to be the product of a deranged mind. Where would it end? Uncontrollable shivers ran across her skin. She finally admitted to herself that she had never been so terrified in her life.

After a few minutes of painfully honest soul-searching, she swallowed her pride and dialed Curtis's number. The hope that he was back from Colorado Springs died when his answering machine came on. His resonant voice on the recording tightened her chest, and she realized how important his support had become.

"It's me, Gail..." she started to leave a message asking him to call when he got home, but pride got in the way. She wasn't going to turn into one of his simpering female clients. He probably got enough of that in his work. She brightened her tone. "Just wondering how your day went...hope your day was a good one. See you tomorrow."

She hung up, blinked back tears of frustration and then dialed Angie's number. As evenly as she could, Gail related what had happened. "Could you possibly come over, Angie? I—I need to be with some-one."

"Heaven preserve us!" swore Angie. "Have you called the police?"

"Yes, I'm sorry to bother you—"

"Shut up, gal. Tony and I are on our way. We'll leave Jimmy with a neighbor. Stay near the phone till we get there."

Gail thought she had herself under control, but when Angie and her husband, Tony, came rushing into the library a few minutes later, she felt like someone laying down a heavy burden. Angie enveloped Gail in a bear hug that squeezed the breath out of her.

"You're okay?" Her dark Italian eyes swept over Gail's ashen face.

Gail managed a weak smile. "Now I am."

Angie wrinkled her nose. "Phew. What a stink."

"I'll take a look," said Tony, a husky, curly-headed Italian who usually was as quiet as Angie was ver-bose. "The back porch...?"

Gail nodded. "Just follow your nose. Don't touch anything...until the police get here."

"From the stink, I don't think I'll be tempted." Tony gave her a wry smile.

"It's pretty awful," Gail felt a sickening lurch in her stomach as she remembered the loathsome sight.

"Kids!" muttered Tony as he went down the hall.

"Do you think it's kids?" Gail asked Angie, over-hearing Tony's mutter.

Angie shook her head. "It's some crazy...it has to be."

A half hour later, when Lieutenant Lamont arrived with two other men, Angie told him the same thing. "Some nut's running around loose... and you've got to stop him. Gail can't take much more of this." She waggled a plump finger at the detective. "You better start taking this business seriously."

Lamont said in a quiet tone that was more ominous than his usual biting tongue, "Yes, I believe we should."

Angie was nonplussed for a second, then she got a second wind. "Well, what are you going to do about it?"

He gave Angie a weary but patient smile. "We'll try to find similarities between this harassment and other incidents of the same kind. Try to find the common denominator and hope it offers a clue to the perpetrator or perpetrators. In other words, we'll be looking for the proverbial needle in a haystack, Mrs. Difalco—but we will be looking."

Angie pursed her mouth. "I suppose that means that Gail's going to have to put up with this revolting torment for God knows how long."

"Angie..." cautioned her husband in a soothing tone, sending an apologetic look at Lamont. "When your men are through taking pictures and collecting evidence, could we start cleaning up?" Tony asked.

"You don't have to do that," protested Gail. She hadn't even thought about getting rid of the obnoxious mess.

When the lieutenant was satisfied the place had been covered as completely as possible, Angie and Tony went in the kitchen to find mops and pails. Lamont pulled a chair close to Gail's and took out his note-book. "Sorry I was slow in getting here. Your call came in about six-thirty?"

She nodded.

"Tell me what happened."

Gail described waking up with the foul smell in her nostrils.

"You were napping in your bedroom?"

She nodded. "I came home tired from therapy..." Then her eyes widened. "Inga!"

"Yes?" he snapped. "Inga? The housekeeper?"

"Yes, the young blond woman who let you in the other day. She must have done it. Her way of getting even with me." Gail's eyes lost their bewildered look and snapped with sudden anger. She told the detective what she'd found when she'd come home from therapy. "I couldn't believe my eyes...Inga was standing in front of the mirror, painted up like a gargoyle and her hair standing out like she'd put her finger in a light socket. I fired her and heard her leave by the back door."

"Leaving it unlocked?"

"I suppose so. Don't you see? She must have come back while I was sleeping."

"What time did you dismiss her?"

"About four-thirty. And I smelled the stench about an hour and a half later. She had plenty of time to get the eggs and chicken guts and come back."

"Really? Where would *you* go on the spur of the moment, Miss Richards, to get a couple of dozen rotten eggs, chicken feathers and guts in a hurry?"

Gail blinked. "I—I don't know."

Lamont's expression was speculative. "An hour and a half isn't much time to prepare that kind of vicious assault. Collecting the stuff would involve some planning. And she'd need more time then she had to go get it and come back."

"But it had to be Inga," she insisted stubbornly. "Maybe she'd planned the whole thing ahead of time. My firing her was really after the fact. I was dissatisfied with her and she knew it. Her manner was abrasive. An unpleasant person to have around. She must have known I wasn't going to keep her." Gail told him what the woman at the employment agency had said about Inga.

"We'll check her out, of course. Now let's go over time and details again."

Gail repeated what time the housekeeper had left and how long she had slept before waking up to the stench. No, she hadn't heard anything, but she'd been extremely tired and fighting a headache. She'd slept heavily. No, there hadn't been any threatening note this time. "Doesn't that prove that this was different from the other incidents?" she challenged. "That it wasn't the same person?"

The detective's expression was noncommittal. His attitude reminded Gail that he was the one *asking* the questions—not *answering* them. His hesitation to accept Inga as the guilty one worried Gail. A known adversary was easier to fight than one who seemed able to slip through the cracks of a house.

"A locksmith will be coming to change the locks on all the doors," she said defiantly. "And I'm going to make sure they're bolted myself." Even though evil swirled around her, threatening to engulf her, she wasn't going to be cowed in her own house.

A flicker of approval crossed his lean face. "And I think a live-in companion might be in order."

Gail stiffened. "Didn't you tell me that in most cases these malicious pranks are an end in themselves?" She firmed her chin. "Well, I have no intention of living in the shadow of a bodyguard."

"Even someone as resilient as you are, Miss Richards, can be worn down by constant torment. We all have our flashpoints, as O'Mallory put it."

"I won't crumple the way Sherrie and Wilhite did— no matter how long this goes on."

Lamont looked at her, his mouth held in a tight line. "I think I ought to tell you, Miss Richards, that we're beginning to suspect that both of those deaths might *not* have been suicides."

Gail's mouth went dry. "You mean, Mrs. Sinclair was right... her daughter didn't give herself an overdose? But you said—"

"I know what I said... but that was before Wilhite's ex-wife brought in the anonymous notes and ugly packages he'd been receiving before his death. Now we're looking at both of those deaths in a different frame of reference. Sherrie Sinclair and Jasper Wilhite had been involved in accidents fatal to small children and both had received repugnant gifts and threatening nursery rhymes—the same kind you've been receiving. Since both of them were unstable emotionally, circumstances seemed to support the theory that they had taken their own lives." Something hard crept into Lamont's eyes. "But their deaths could have been murder set up to look like suicide."

Gail's hands tightened on the arm of her chair.

"We'll be searching for anything and anybody that is common to the three of you. I want a list of people... anyone who has contact with you."

"It can't be anyone I know," she protested.

"Unfortunately, Miss Richards, I'd bet that's exactly who it is."

THE WOMAN SAT in the bathtub, vigorously soaping herself. A smile played on her lips, satisfied that she left her calling card in good fashion. For days, the fancy house would smell to high heaven as a reminder that Gail Richards was going to pay. *Mama won't let her forget, Robbie.*

She cupped water in her hands and let it run over her head and face. Then she began singing, "Three blind mice...see how they run...they all run after the farmer's wife...she cuts off their tails with a carving knife. Did you ever see such a sight in your life...?"

Laughing, she leaned her head back against the tub, welcoming a deep sense of contentment. The slithering torment of the unrelenting serpent had been stilled, but she knew that the peace within her was only temporary. The guilty woman must pay with her life, but first she must suffer the terror of a trapped animal unable to escape a relentless predator. Stalking her victim brought an exhilaration that swelled her senses and sent bursts of adrenaline coursing through her body.

The child killer was showing signs of stress. Maybe next time it wouldn't be just chicken blood spread all over the floor. She hadn't decided. She knew that when the time was right, she would take the final revenge. Her smile faded and tears began to drip down her cheeks. "Robbie...Robbie."

Chapter Thirteen

Gail managed a few hours sleep, but not in her own bed. She couldn't bring herself to suffer the horrid back bedroom, especially when the repugnant odors lingered in that part of the house despite efforts to air it out. Angie and Tony had carried the offensive boxes out to a storage shed and had scrubbed the walls and floor of the porch. It was after eleven o'clock when they finally left, giving up on trying to get Gail to spend the night somewhere else.

"I'm not being driven out of my own home." *I'll get through this somehow without turning my life into a nightmare.*

"You're one pigheaded woman," Angie had retorted. "I've a mind to stay here whether you like it or not."

"Take her home, Tony," ordered Gail. "She bosses me around all day...I need some peace at night."

Angie snorted and gave Gail a hug. "Sure you'll be all right?"

Gail nodded. "Show's over for tonight. I'll get the locks changed tomorrow and see if Mrs. Rosales is ready to come back."

"Maybe you ought to call O'Mallory...tell him what happened."

"He's out of town," she said flatly. She already thought about giving him another call and lacked the courage to find out if he was back. He might have decided to spend the night in Colorado Springs—alone or with someone else. Gail doubted that such an eligible bachelor ever lacked company. Anyway, she had no claims upon his time. "I'll tell Curtis when I see him tomorrow."

ABOUT THE SAME TIME that Gail turned off the lights and was trying to get settled on the sitting room sofa, Curtis reached the outskirts of Denver on Interstate 25. He'd driven slightly over the speed limit the whole seventy-nine miles back to Denver. His evening meeting had dragged on until ten o'clock, and he'd fidgeted impatiently, glancing at his watch and speculating whether he could get back in time to see Gail. There was a sudden hollowness in him that was beyond anything he'd ever felt before. His thoughts had swung to her like iron filings toward a magnet. Despite every effort to concentrate on the business at hand, he hadn't been able to stop thinking about her. Several times, he had cursed himself for not leaving a number where he could be reached if she needed him. Once he'd tried to call and got a busy signal.

As he turned the corner on her street, his tires squealed and he didn't slow down until he braked in front of her house. The hall light was on, but the house was shrouded in darkness. Moonlight played upon the high mansard roof and bathed the old house in a quiet serenity. The tranquil scene mocked an un-named urgency that had been driving him. His hands were sweaty on the steering wheel. Tense back muscles protested the rigid posture he'd maintained the whole day.

What should he do now? Go ring the doorbell just to reassure himself? Disturb her just to satisfy himself that she was all right? He allowed himself a wry smile. He could just imagine her indignation. She had made it plain that she hated being fussed over.

He sighed, shifted gears and slowly drove away. Then he speeded up. Maybe she'd left a message on his answering machine.

THE NIGHT was a long one for Gail. After a couple of hours her back protested the softness of the cushions. Near dawn she wrapped herself in a quilt, sat in the wing chair and watched gray muted light outline the edges of her new drapes. She couldn't stop thinking about Sherrie Sinclair and Jasper Wilhite. Maybe they hadn't committed suicide. Gail leaned her head back against the chair and closed her eyes. Maybe they had been murdered. She fought back a rising nausea. *By somebody they knew.*

No, she wouldn't believe it. Living in constant sus-picion of everyone and everything went against every fiber of her being. How could she cower like a hunted animal, fearful behind locked doors and terrified in her own home? She would take all the precautions she could. Every day she was getting stronger physically.

In a defiant gesture, she got up and pulled back the fringed draperies. The sky was luminous with a pink glow, promising a cloudless Colorado day. She stood in the frame of the windows for a long time. Then she turned away. "I'm going to get my life back!" The resolve firmed the lines of her mouth. She walked without the aid of her cane to the back of the house, relieved that the horrid odor was gone. She dressed quickly in a pretty blue wool dress with matching jacket and took time to put her hair in a French braid. There wasn't anything she could do about the faint shadows under her eyes, but she was satisfied that she presented the appearance of a woman in control of her life.

Right after breakfast, she checked with the locksmith and ordered dead-bolt locks for both doors. "Please try to install them today if possible." Then she called the Happy Household office and reported that she'd fired Inga Neilson for inappropriate behavior.

The woman sighed. "I wanted to give Inga a second chance, but I guess we'll have to drop her from our list."

"You mean she's been dismissed before?"

"I'm afraid so. . . she didn't work out as a nanny. I thought she might do better at housekeeping."

Gail tried to elicit more information about Inga from the woman, but she wouldn't add anything more to what she'd already said. Lieutenant Lamont would be more successful, thought Gail. Mrs. Rosales was working another assignment but would be able to come back to Gail in a couple of days.

"Would you like to have another temporary?"

"No," said Gail quickly. "I'll manage."

A few minutes later, Curtis called from his office. "You've been on the phone all morning, Miss Richards," he chided her.

His wonderfully warm voice washed over her and set off a foolish inner tingling. "So you're back."

"Got back about eleven-thirty last night. Came by your house, but everything was wrapped up for the night."

Gail hesitated and decided against saying anything about last night's vandalism. He'd find out about the latest ugliness soon enough. The house was finally free of the awful smell and she wanted to put it all behind her. "Checking up on me?" she teased.

"You might call it that. Or maybe I just had the urge to see you." His voice deepened. "I kept thinking about you yesterday...the whole day was a waste. What do you say I bring Scuffy over for her lesson at one? Then I can bring the two of you back to the center for therapy. We can talk about Friday night."

"What's Friday night?"

"That's what we'll talk about," he promised with a chuckle.

ANGIE WAS RELIEVED to find Gail in such good spirits. "You're amazing, gal. You got more resiliency than a rubber band. Don't know how you do it. If someone had done that to my house, I'd be in bed with a bottle of aspirin."

"No, you wouldn't," retorted Gail, laughing. "You'd be sitting on the front porch with a shotgun."

"Not a bad idea. You still think it was Inga?"

"I called the employment agency this morning. The woman wasn't surprised that I'd fired Inga. She said something interesting. She was trying to give Inga a second chance because she hadn't worked out as a nanny. I find that very surprising."

"Why?"

"Because of the way she reacted to Jimmy. Playing with him was the only time I ever saw an animated expression on her face. Remember? She was actually laughing instead of scowling. I would have thought she'd make a much better nanny than a housekeeper. I wonder what went wrong that she lost the job."

"Maybe because of the same kind of weird behavior," offered Angie. "Anyway, good riddance, I say. She'd have to be off her rocker to get revenge by trashing your house like that."

When Miss Crum arrived for Scuffy's lesson, Gail had the unpleasant task of informing the bouncing plump lady that she had decided to tutor the little girl herself. Angie kept her distance, watching the confrontation with snapping dark eyes.

"But I spent a lot of time preparing a cute little bingo game for today," protested the blue-eyed lady. "See." She held out a box filled with homemade cards. "I draw a letter and Scuffy puts a marker on the picture that starts with that letter." The teacher's round pink face glowed.

"Doesn't Scuffy already know her beginning sounds?" questioned Gail.

"Well, I—I don't know. I just thought—"

"Didn't you give her the diagnostic tests that Mrs. Difalco laid out?" Gail asked, smiling, trying to take the edge off the question. "They usually give us a pretty good idea where the problems are."

Edith Crum's mouth thinned, and the woman's usually bubbly, sugar-coated voice became quite scratchy. "I don't think it hurts to review the first few lessons. I spent nearly twenty years teaching first graders to read, Miss Richards."

Angie shot Gail a look that said Oh boy, here we go!

The teacher thrust her chubby face closer to Gail's. Her double chin quivered. "I think I'm qualified to make my own lesson plans."

"I'm sure that you're an excellent teacher, Mrs. Crum, but our program is different from that offered in a regular classroom," explained Gail in a reasonable tone.

Miss Crum tossed her curly head. "I never had a principal who didn't give me the highest rating. No one has ever questioned my methods of teaching."

Gail tried a conciliatory smile. "We try to offer different approaches to students who have failed with traditional methods. I think you'll find our individualized instruction very—"

"Cold and mechanical," the teacher flared, finishing the sentence. "I saw from the first that you were trying to treat human beings like machines." She drew herself up to her full five-foot height. "I don't want any part of it. You should look to your conscience, Miss Richards. These people come to you for help—not exploitation! I think the State Board of Education should be made aware of what goes on here."

"The Learning House is duly licensed," Angie flared, unable to keep her silence any longer. "I suggest you get yourself out of here, lady. I'm the one that hired you…and I'm the one firing you!'' Angie waved the woman out of the room and dogged her footsteps all the way down the hall.

Gail slammed down a folder. Criticism of her reading program was harder on her than any personal attack. She prided herself on the success of her individualized instruction. In a few months her students gained a year or more in their reading level, and she had confidence in her eclectic approach. If it hadn't been for the accident— A sense of despair swept over Gail with such force that she felt that she was drowning in it. If Edith Crum spread rumors to the media, the Learning House would be ruined.

''Well, good riddance, I'd say,'' said Angie, coming back and dusting off her hands in a satisfied gesture. ''I didn't want to worry you earlier, but she refused to use our materials. I could see that the students were getting turned off. I'm not surprised our enrollment dropped like a runaway elevator. Just listening to her saccharine do-gooder voice made me sick to my stomach. And underneath she wasn't all that sweet. Just let one of the kids argue and her eyes turned granite. Yesterday, she looked ready to stuff Scuffy in a bucket of water more than once.''

Gail glanced at her watch. ''Speaking of Scuffy, I wonder where she is. Curtis said he was going to bring her over. It's already one o'clock. We need to start her lesson on time if I'm going to make my therapy session.''

Angie made a disapproving sound with her tongue. ''You're trying to do too much. I'm betting you didn't get more than a couple of hours of sleep after that business last night." She looked worried. "I don't know what to expect next."

Gail smiled at her sheepishly. "Well, we've fired the housekeeper and our substitute teacher...I don't think there's anyone else we can give the ax to."

They both laughed and for a moment it was like old times. When they had first started the center, they had been buried in problems but they had worked them through. They had learned to meet each crisis head-on. And they'd become good friends.

"I'll call the teachers' registry and see if I can find another sub. One that doesn't think of herself as Little Bo-Peep." Angie frowned. "Now why did I say that?" She shrugged and reached for the phone.

It rang before she could pick it up.

"Learning Center...no, she's not here. We were wondering if she was going to show up for her lesson...yes...yes...just a minute." Angie handed Gail the phone.

"Hi, me again," said Curtis. "Just checking to see if Scuffy's there."

"No. I thought you were going to bring her over. Is there a problem?"

Curtis gave a short laugh. "With Scuffy there's always a problem. She swiped old man Whittier's electric wheelchair while he was in X-ray."

"You're kidding."

"I wish I were. The chair was sitting in the hall and she took off with it. One of the outpatients saw her roaring out a side door at full speed, her crutches propped in the seat beside her and her red hair whipping in the breeze.''

The picture was all too clear, and Gail couldn't help laughing. Leave it to Scuffy to turn a wheelchair into a hot rod.

"We've had people out looking for a half an hour. She's nowhere on the grounds," said Curtis. "I had an idea she might show up at your place. It's only a few blocks and she knows the way. I thought she might have decided to come by herself. Call me if she shows up."

Gail assured him that she would and hung up the phone, chuckling. "That little minx. Scuffy's run off with some fellow's electric wheelchair. Curtis thought she might have come here on her own."

"Not likely." Angie laughed. "I bet that kid's headed for the nearest McDonald's on Colorado Boulevard. Probably causing a traffic snarl while she zooms across the street in perfect innocence." Angie shook her dark head. "Sure glad she's not my responsibility."

"I guess we can forget about any lesson today." Gail had to admit she was disappointed. She had wanted to show Scuffy that she could read if she'd apply herself. That bright little mind of hers was going to waste . . . except when trouble presented itself.

"I suppose I'd better put this stuff back." Angie started picking up material that Gail had planned to use. "Go put your feet up and rest till Mr. O'Mallory comes."

"You're an angel."

"So I've been told. Now go."

Gail walked slowly down the hall toward her sitting room, leaning more heavily on her cane than she liked. She'd managed to get a morning nap but she still felt tired.

She paused in front of the front glass doors, looking through the small vestibule to the outside door. What if Scuffy had come to the house and been unable to navigate the front steps by herself?

When Gail opened the front door, she wouldn't have been surprised to see the little girl sitting there, scowling at her, but there wasn't any sign of Scuffy or of the commandeered wheelchair. Unless she was on the driveway? Gail pushed on the screen door to open it wider but something held it.

A sickening nausea flipped her stomach. *Another package?* Her first impulse was to draw back and slam the door on whatever lay against it, but fury overcame her apprehension. She gave the screen door a vicious shove, and something slithered across the porch into view.

She screamed.

The object was a child's crutch—one end covered with fresh blood.

CURTIS GOT THERE as fast as he could. "It's Scuffy's crutch, all right." His face was blanched of color as he came into the sitting room. "I've notified the police. Is that where you found it?"

"I pushed on the screen door and...and it slid across the porch." Gail's voice sounded too far away to be her own.

"But you didn't see any sign of Scuffy... or the wheelchair?"

She blinked back a sudden fullness in her eyes. "No, just the crutch." Her eyes pleaded for reassurance. "What happened to her?"

"Maybe nothing."

"But—"

"She's probably perfectly all right," he said firmly. "Knowing Scuffy, she'll have a good laugh on all of us."

"But the blood—"

"That doesn't mean it's hers." He tried to smile but his eyes remained grim.

He walked over to the front window and then back again. "I feel as if I should be doing something... but I don't want to disturb any evidence the police might pick up." He turned to Angie as she came in. "You didn't see anything, did you?"

Angie sent an anxious glance at Gail. "No. I heard Gail scream and came running. I stepped out on the porch... but didn't see anything but the crutch." Her voice quavered slightly. "What do you make of it?"

"I don't know," he admitted. "It isn't past Scuffy to do something like this to get everybody worked up."

"What if it's another torment...intended for me?" Gail clenched her hands tightly in her lap.

Curtis touched her shoulder. "Steady. Don't jump to conclusions. An unfortunate coincidence, that's all. You're having more than your share."

"Well, it's got to stop!" fumed Angie. "After that business last night—"

"What business?" demanded Curtis, his eyes sharply alert.

Gail pressed her fingers against throbbing temples and let Angie tell him about the foul desecration by rotten eggs and chicken entrails.

"I knew it!" said Curtis. "I couldn't get rid of an uneasy feeling that I needed to get back to town and reassure myself that everything was all right. I pushed the speed limit all the way back. Damn. I should have followed my instincts." He ran a hand through his wavy hair. "Why didn't you call me?"

"I did...earlier in the evening. And then I decided...not to bother you—"

"Bother me!" He wanted at once to shake her, kiss her and lift her up in his arms and carry her off like some modern Lochinvar.

"She's stubborn," offered Angie.

"Tell me something I don't know. I've never met such an exasperating female in my life." His caressing look defused the criticism. She was so damn appealing that it hurt.

Officers Kline and Mantelli arrived and began asking questions. Curtis and Angie both identified the crutch as Scuffy's because of purple nail polish splattered on the handle.

"I teased her about it," said Angie. "She admitted spilling the ugly polish all over everything. Said the head nurse, Mrs. Tewsberry, was fit to be tied. Apparently more than her crutches got splattered with the horrible color."

"And the last time she was seen?"

"About twelve," said Curtis. "She left the center in an electric wheelchair. We've had staff out looking for her. I called here because she was due for a tutoring lesson at one o'clock."

"And she never showed?" asked Mantelli. His dark eyes settled on Gail.

"No. Mr. O'Mallory called a little after one to tell us she was missing."

"Did anybody else come in or go out of the house about that time?" Officer Kline asked.

Gail and Angie exchanged glances. *Edith Crum!*

Gail nodded. "A substitute teacher."

While Angie told the officers about the heated scene that resulted in Edith Crum's dismissal, Gail's thoughts began to race. Had the irate teacher run into Scuffy on her way out? Surely she wouldn't have taken her rage out on a child—unless Scuffy had provoked her beyond reason.

"I'll get her address and phone number," said Angie, heading toward the door. Gail could tell Angie was satisfied in her own mind that Edith Crum had some part in the mystery.

"We have an APB out on the little girl," said Officer Kline. "If she's riding around in a wheelchair, she won't be hard to spot."

"No sign of wheelchair tracks on the sidewalk out front, but the cement's dry," offered Mantelli.

Kline closed his notebook. "We'll take a close look around." He gave Gail the hint of a teasing grin. "We know our way around."

She flushed. Privacy had been something she had treasured and protected. She had avoided calling attention to herself even in the most benign situations. She recoiled from the truth that her name on a police blotter had become a familiar one. How long would it be before the officers concluded that she was the one responsible for the demands on their time?

Curtis read the anguish in her eyes. "Come on. You're going to lie down and rest. Don't argue." He helped her to her feet. "Don't even think about going to the center today. You need rest more than exercise."

Gail was surprised how easy it was to give in to his dictates. *I must be tired*, she thought, *letting him order me around like this*. She hid a secret smile. It was kind of nice, in fact.

They had reached the kitchen, when Officer Kline came bursting in the back door. "We found the wheelchair...half buried in the snow near the garage. No sign of the kid." He grabbed the phone and gave crisp orders for more officers. "We'll need to launch an intensive search of grounds and house," he told someone.

Curtis saw Gail's ashen face. "Better if you stay out of the way. Lie down. I'll let you know..."

If they find her. The unfinished sentence vibrated painfully in Gail's head as Curtis followed the officer out the back door. A wave of weakness forced her to concentrate on every muscle she used to put one foot in front of the other as she left the kitchen and headed down the back hall. Voices rang in her ears, doors opened and closed and loud footsteps vibrated through the house. A sense of panic was like a relentless surf rising higher and higher.

When she reached the small bedroom, she started across the floor to her bed, but her eyes were drawn to the old Victorian wardrobe. Several pieces of cloth were caught in the door, keeping it from closing completely. It hadn't been that way when she'd dressed that morning.

No one else had been in this part of the house.

Dizziness blurred her vision. Sudden sharp pain radiated behind her eyes. As if some sixth sense had already delivered a shattering message, she reached forward and pulled on the ornate door handle.

The little girl's body was crumpled in a grotesque heap in the small space. Her head had fallen sideways, with only the whites of her eyes showing. Blood oozed from a raw wound on the side of her head and left ugly streaks down her freckled cheeks.

Gail screamed.

Chapter Fourteen

Gail couldn't remember who answered her screams, or who rushed in and led her into the bathroom to be sick. Voices, sirens, loud footsteps and the creak of an ambulance gurney barely registered as she hovered on the edge of consciousness.

Soothing hands pushed back sweat-drenched hair falling over her face. Then Curtis's strong arms lifted her up, carried her through the house and up the stairs. When he laid her on her own bed, the familiar scent of her pillows and the bed's remembered comfort brought grateful tears to her eyes. She tried to say something but couldn't control shudders rippling from head to toe.

"More blankets, Angie," ordered Curtis. "Her skin is clammy."

"The doctor's on his way. How about some brandy?"

Curtis shook his head. "Better not. Alcohol might not be the best thing for shock."

He tucked the covers tightly around her. Then he slipped his arm under her head and shoulders and held her close. The warmth of his body spread to hers. He touched his lips to her moist forehead and murmured reassurances. "It's all right, sweet lady."

"Scuffy..." she croaked. The horrible sight swept over her again.

"They've taken her to emergency."

She's not dead?

Curtis read the question in her anguished eyes. "There was a faint heartbeat."

Gail closed her eyes against the memory of those sightless eyes and the blood-streaked face. The child's head had been twisted at an awkward angle like a rag doll's. Gail shivered and Curtis tightened his embrace. She buried her face gratefully in his shoulder.

"Scuffy's a tough little kid. She'll make it, you'll see." He wished he believed his own words, but he had seen how lifeless her little body was when they'd taken her out on the gurney. "It's a good thing you found her when you did."

Angie came in, glanced at Gail's ashen face and blinked back tears in her own eyes. "Dear God in heaven, why couldn't it have been me that found her? Gail hasn't had a chance to get her strength back after the accident. All those horrible things happening. No wonder she's going to pieces—"

"Cut it out, Angie," Curtis ordered. "Gail's *not* going to pieces. She's had a shock, that's all. Anyone would have a similar reaction."

Gail lifted her head and tried to send Angie a reassuring smile, but the attempt was less than successful. Her friend looked as worried as ever.

"I—I don't understand," Angie stammered, wringing her hands. "How could it have happened?

We were in the house all the time. How could the child end up in Gail's wardrobe?''

Curtis's mouth was tight. ''Because someone deliberately set it up so Gail was the most likely one to find her . . . dead.''

''But why?'' Angie's eyes suddenly widened. ''You think it's the same crazy who's been doing the other stuff?''

Curtis's look was grim. ''I'd bet on it. Only this time it's not fun and games.'' To himself he added, *This time it's attempted murder.*

Angie gave Gail a worried glance as she turned and left.

The shock of finding Scuffy had begun to lessen, leaving Gail in a kind of detached state. She was cradled in the curve of Curtis's shoulders and felt his lips touching her hairline with soft, reassuring kisses. When the doctor came, he gave Gail a sedative and agreed with Curtis that a round-the-clock nurse be engaged for at least the next couple of days and nights. He left orders that Gail was to remain in bed until she got over the emotional trauma.

''It's a shame,'' he told Curtis out in the hall. ''She's one gallant little lady. I hate to see her put through something like this. Doesn't seem fair.''

After the doctor had gone, Curtis sat on the edge of the bed looking at Gail's wan face as she slept. Love, admiration and deep worry knotted his heart strings. She wasn't like any woman he'd ever known. She was so feminine and appealing, her strength like a lovely flower pushing up through the cracks in hard rock. He was astounded by the demands she had put on herself to regain her physical strength and her indomitable will to be independent.

He bent over and kissed her closed eyelids and laid his cheek softly against hers. He knew then how precious she had become to him.

LIEUTENANT LAMONT arrived at the house with four men. He accompanied them in and out of the house, slicing the air with his quick hands as he snapped out orders.

Curtis stayed out of the way, waiting for the opportunity to lay his demands in front of the detective. He was ready to do battle and was filled with an impatience that was difficult to keep in check. Gail was going to get some police protection—now!

He swore when he saw a television van pull up in front of the house. Two people spilled out the doors, a female reporter and photographer with his bulky camera equipment. The fellow began taking sweeps of the house with his camera, lingering on the small white-and-black sign Learning House that Gail had placed on the front lawn. The agile, pretty woman with a notebook began writing busily as they approached the house. They stopped at a yellow band the police had stretched across the front steps. The photograph zeroed in on the bloody crutch still lying on the porch. The woman reporter shouted questions at one of the officers, who just shook his head.

Curtis could hardly restrain himself from marching out and ordering them off the property. He shuddered to think what the news story would do to Gail's business. The publicity could ruin her.

After a few minutes, the news team disappeared around the house and Curtis's worst fears were realized when he saw the reporter and cameraman take up a position on top of a shed where they could see everything going on in the backyard. The photographer took pictures of the half-buried wheelchair and of Lamont's men searching the grounds all the way around the house.

Suddenly a shout went up from an officer. He'd found the other crutch shoved under the back step. The TV team got it all, and Curtis knew he would be able to see the gory details on the five o'clock news.

More than an hour later, everyone but Lamont had left. The detective came in the kitchen, sat down at the kitchen table, made some notes and then asked about Gail.

"In shock. The doctor gave her a sedative," Curtis told him. "Angie Difalco is with her until a nurse arrives."

Lamont nodded approval.

"What do you think happened?" asked Curtis.

The detective gave his glasses a shove. "From the physical evidence, I'd speculate that the victim was hit on the head with her crutch near the front steps. Wheelchair tracks are visible on the east side of the house and around to the back. Looks as though the girl was carried into the house through the back door, put in the wardrobe and then the wheelchair was run into the snowbank. One crutch was stuffed under the back stairs . . . the other left on the front porch—"

"For Gail to find," finished Curtis angrily. "It's more of the same kind of harassment . . . only this time the life of a little girl may have been sacrificed. How could anyone brutalize a child like that? This psychotic has got to be stopped!''

Lamont flipped the pages of his notebook without responding to Curtis's emotional tirade. ''The call about the girl being gone from the center came in about twelve-thirty. Is that correct?''

Curtis reined in his emotions. It wouldn't do any good to make Lamont a scapegoat for his fears. He nodded. ''I heard about it about fifteen minutes after it happened. I called Gail to see if Scuffy had come to the house by herself but she hadn't. My secretary and I joined a couple of aides and orderlies who were out hunting for her.''

''The call for an ambulance came in at approximately one twenty-eight. A time window of less than an hour. Pretty damn short. Someone had to know the house and move quickly—and efficiently.''

''You think it was all planned ahead of time?''

The lieutenant looked over his glasses at Curtis. ''Not likely. Let's be reasonable. The whole thing must have developed spontaneously...on the spot. A kid stealing an electric wheelchair is not something anyone would predict. But when the situation presented itself, someone was ready to take advantage of it.''

''But why?''

''If I knew that, I'd be ready to go for an arrest warrant.''

Angie came into the kitchen and Curtis started to get up. ''Gail?'' he asked anxiously.

She waved him down. ''The nurse is here. Gail's still sleeping.''

Lamont held out a chair. "I'd like to ask you a few questions if you wouldn't mind, Mrs. Difalco," he requested smoothly. The invitation was nicely put, but his sharp black eyes indicated there wasn't any real choice.

Curtis listened as Angie explained that the substitute teacher had arrived shortly before one o'clock for Scuffy's reading lesson. "Gail fired her because she refused to follow the prescribed tests and materials. The woman stomped out, threatening to have the center investigated."

"What time?"

"About five minutes after one, I'd guess."

"So if the crutch had been against the door at that time, she would have seen it?"

Angie's eyes widened. "You don't think that she—?"

"I let the evidence do my thinking. I'll want Edith Crum's address and telephone number. Anyone else in the house? I know she dismissed Inga Neilson. Did she engage someone else?"

Angie shook her head. "Gail called the agency, but the woman she wanted, Mrs. Rosales, was working somewhere else for a couple more days. You don't think that Inga—"

Lamont ignored the question. He went over some of the same ground again, then stuffed his notebook in his pocket. "Thank you. That's all for now."

"Wait a minute, Lieutenant." Curtis stopped his quick departure from the room. "You can't say that Gail doesn't need protection after what happened today. I insist you assign an officer to stay in the house with her." His tone was loud and belligerent.

Lamont gave a short wave of his hand and said over his shoulder, "Sgt. Betty Rossini should be here within the hour."

Angie laughed at Curtis's ready-to-do-battle expression. "All you need is a horse and shield...a modern knight protecting his lady love." Then she sobered. "I can tell Gail's taken with you. And she has a pretty tight lock on her heart."

"I know."

"I'm usually right about men and can tell a womanizer a mile off," bragged Angie. "But my record isn't perfect. If I'm wrong about you, Curtis O'Mallory, and you're taking advantage of Gail's vulnerability, I'll personally see you torn limb from limb."

He smiled at her bulldog expression. "Angie, you don't need to worry about my feelings. It's Gail I'm worried about. When all this is over, she may show me the door in quick order."

Angie thought for a minute, and then sighed. "Sometimes that gal is just too damn independent."

Curtis refused to leave until satisfied that Gail was in good hands with a brisk, motherly nurse attending to her needs and a female officer securing the house.

Sergeant Rossini was a solid woman of medium height with quick, intelligent eyes. Somewhere in her late thirties, she'd been on the force for nearly fifteen years. Rossini called the locksmith and had him on the job within an hour. Curtis left the house with a growing sense of relief. When he had phoned the hospital, the report about Scuffy's condition had been noncommittal, so he drove to St. Joseph's Hospital and was informed that the little girl was in surgery.

"Severe concussion. No, she hadn't regained consciousness. Prognosis uncertain."

He knew there wasn't anything he could do. The intensive care waiting room was full of people waiting for loved ones to be brought up from surgery. A couple of men were watching a small TV in the room. Curtis couldn't hear the sound, but he could see the screen. A pretty blond reporter was relating the news. She was standing in front of Gail's house and the camera was offering pictures of the bloody crutch and snow-covered wheelchair.

Curtis left the hospital and went to his health club. Swearing and clenching his jaw, he savagely batted a boxing bag until he couldn't raise his arms anymore.

THE FIVE-O'CLOCK NEWS blared through the small house as the woman sat on the floor in front of the television. She was changing clothes on a round-faced baby doll. A contented smile played on her face as she smoothed out the tiny ruffled dress. The doll's blue eyes opened and closed as she tipped it back and forth.

"See-saw Margery Daw.
Baby shall have a new master.
She shall have a slap on the face
Because she can't work any faster."

She laughed and battered the doll from side to side with her broad hand as she sang. She gave a sideways glance at the TV screen and stopped abruptly.

Her eyes narrowed in concentration as she listened to the account of a small girl found stuffed in a cupboard at the Learning House, a private reading center owned and operated by Gail Richards. According to reliable sources, the pretty reporter told her audience, the child had arrived in an electric wheelchair and been struck on the head with her own crutch. She was still alive but in critical condition at a local hospital.

The woman frowned.

Several more shots were shown of the wheelchair and one of a policeman pulling the crutch out from under the back stairs.

"Miss Richards was not available for comment but it was learned that she is recovering from an automobile accident in which a teenage boy was killed. At the moment, Miss Richards is not considered a suspect, but the police have closed the Learning House, pending further investigation."

With a whoop of joy, the woman flung the doll high in the air. It came down with a crash that cracked its porcelain face and knocked the blue eyes back in its head.

For a long moment, the woman just stared at it. Her expression was empty as she picked it up, stared at the empty sockets and fingered the jagged cracks. Then she began to savagely pull off the arms and legs, twisting the neck until it broke and the battered head lay in her hand.

She walked out the back door, clutching the dismembered doll, and with a shovel scooped out enough dirt to bury the doll. When she was finished, she went in the house and brought out a plastic rose. She stuck it in the ground, bowed her head and let tears run down her face.

Chapter Fifteen

Gail was on her feet again in less than twenty-four hours. With the nurse on one side of her and Sergeant Rossini on the other, she navigated the stairs safely up and down to her second-floor bedroom. Gail was determined not to lose the strength she'd worked so hard to gain, and she only missed one day of therapy.

After a couple of nights, the nurse was dismissed and Sergeant Rossini was put on night shift only. The officer came at dusk and left when Mrs. Rosales arrived in the morning at seven o'clock. Angie continued to put in her hours every day, even though there were no students coming to the house.

"A good time to clean out some of the files," she announced in her breezy way. "We'll have everything shipshape when we open the doors for business again."

Gail appreciated her friend's optimism, but she had seen the ugly accounts in the newspaper. Mrs. Karbough had called to say she was utterly appalled to think that such a thing could have happened where *her* son was a student. She informed Gail in haughty tones that she was withdrawing Keith immediately. Day after day, the computers remained silent, the reading rooms empty and the house locked up against intruders.

Anger fueled Gail's determination to regain her health, her reputation and her business. She drove herself relentlessly, staying at Crestview for most of the day. She exercised, swam and chalked up miles on the walking machine. No one could get her to slow down. Curtis tried, but she wouldn't let up.

He made a habit of stopping by the therapy rooms every day at quitting time. Gail's face would be luminous with beads of sweat, her forehead marred with deep furrows of concentration and her jaw would be clenched fiercely. She'd nod at him and go on doing exercises on the mat or lifting weights until she looked ready to collapse.

One afternoon he couldn't stand watching her whip herself one more minute. He turned off her exercising machine. "Enough is enough."

She was furious. "I know when I'm ready to quit."

"No, you don't," he countered firmly.

Curtis talked to Gail's doctor. "She can't keep up this pace."

"I checked her over last week. She's making astonishing progress. I wish I had another dozen patients just like her."

Curtis held his tongue. The doctor wouldn't have said that if he had known the furies driving her. Gail was never relaxed. She wore a guarded expression when they passed the bloodstains on the porch. No matter where they were, he had felt her body become tense, alert to any threatening sound or movement.

Her every sense seemed to be alert to unseen danger. Night and day, like a hunted animal, she waited.

Curtis wanted to reassure her that she was perfectly safe, but he couldn't. Lamont had followed all the leads and had come up empty-handed. Curtis knew that Sergeant Rossini couldn't be assigned to the house indefinitely.

"Surely you have some clues? Some hint about the psychology of the assailant," Curtis badgered the detective.

"We can't be sure of anything. It's only my gut feeling that all the incidents involving Miss Richards are related. Our psychiatrist has offered a vague personality sketch drawn from the nursery rhymes. Probably a woman...most likely suffering from a maternal fixation and deep frustration. Could be she's lost a child or wants one desperately."

"That's it?"

He nodded.

"But that doesn't make sense. Why would someone with a maternal fixation try to kill a little girl like Scuffy?"

"Doesn't add up, does it?" agreed Lamont. "But if we had the whole picture, it might. Crime is like a jigsaw puzzle. To understand it, you have to have all the pieces."

Curtis thought about the analogy the rest of the day.

"You're awfully quiet tonight," Gail said as they were driving home from the hospital. There had been no change in Scuffy's condition. The little girl had been in a coma for more than two weeks and her condition remained critical.

"I talked with Lamont today," said Curtis.

Gail didn't even ask him what progress they'd made in finding Scuffy's attacker. She knew—none.

"He's still working on the theory that it's someone who has a common bond with Sherrie, Wilhite and you."

"I know he's been checking up on Inga, Edith Crum, Angie and Mrs. Rosales. Who else is there?"

"Somebody at Crestview?"

"Didn't they give everyone the third degree when Larry was killed?"

He nodded. "But maybe they were looking for the wrong piece or asking the wrong questions."

The wrong piece. Gail leaned her head back against the car seat. She had been over everything so many times that her memories were threadbare. She'd looked at each incident from myriad directions and always with the same result—her thoughts whirled like a distorted kaleidoscope. Only one thing remained clear. The danger was still out there. Waiting and watching.

When they reached Gail's house, Curtis put his arm around her waist as they walked slowly to the door. The temptation was strong to draw on his caring concern and accept without reservation that something wonderful had happened between them, but Gail didn't trust her own feelings. And she was suspicious of his.

He took her new key and unlocked the front door. They stepped inside the foyer and through the glass doors, they could see Sergeant Rossini standing in the hall waiting.

"A little like being in a goldfish bowl, isn't it?" quipped Curtis as he drew Gail close. She gave herself up to the warmth of his embrace and let his mouth capture hers in a lingering gentle good-night kiss. Then she drew away rather stiffly.

"Don't be self-conscious, sweetheart. Rossini has seen a man in love before."

Gail knew that it wasn't the time or place, but the words were out before she could swallow them back. "Are you sure it's love—and not something else?"

"What on earth are you talking about?"

Gail's pride drove her on. "You could be feeling sorry for me. And because of the circumstances, you want to take care of me...."

"Of course I want to take care of you, silly one. I love you."

"I don't think love that grows out of pity or sympathy is very enduring."

If she had slapped him, he couldn't have been more dumbfounded. His impulse was to shake her and kiss her and carry her off to bed. A night of passionate lovemaking would speak for itself, but that was out of the question at the moment. Even though he was angry, hurt and frustrated, he reined in his emotion and let his counselor's training come to the front. He rephrased her words. "You are afraid that my feelings for you arise out of sympathy, is that it?"

"Yes. And I couldn't take that."

"And how do I prove that they don't arise out of anything but a desire to be with you, to touch you and share your hopes and dreams?"

She moistened her lips. "I don't think we should make any firm commitments until I'm fully well again...and things are back to normal. You might not like me when I'm myself—and not someone you feel you have to guard and protect."

"I could argue that point, but for the moment I accept your reasoning. No long-term commitments—just short-term." He grinned, pulled her close and kissed her again. This time there was an urgent hunger that deepened the pressure of his lips, tugging, working, tasting until she drew away breathless and trembling.

Her eyes were liquid pools of green and her mouth soft and expectant. She'd have a hard time believing that pity was responsible for the passion flashing like summer lightning between them, he thought with secret satisfaction. He smiled silently to himself as he opened the glass doors for her to pass.

CRESTVIEW Rehabilitation Center was silent as Curtis walked down the empty hall to his office a few minutes later. The patient rooms were on the second floor and the administration offices, the cafeteria and therapy rooms were on the first. All the business doors were closed and locked for the night and faint sounds echoed down the empty hall. Curtis let himself in his darkened office and turned on a small light over Myra's desk.

For a moment he hesitated. What he planned to do was wrong and he knew it. There'd be hell to pay if he were caught. He'd never taken lightly the principles of ethical behavior and had always prided himself that rational thought and not emotions had governed his actions—until now.

His body was still suffused with the warmth of holding Gail in his arms. This was the woman that he wanted in his life, and he knew that he would gamble more than just his reputation in order to protect her from the evil that was distorting her life with ugliness.

He opened the drawers on Myra's desk, searching through them until he found a set of keys. Myra needed access to the computer room and business offices to do her job, and the keys were all nicely labeled. Dropping them into his pocket, he turned out the light, quietly closed the door of his office and walked purposefully down the hall to the front of the building.

So far, so good, he thought as he reached the personnel office. He paused, listening. The cleaning crew started at the business offices each night and worked their way to the back of the building. He calculated that they should have reached the cafeteria by now, which was midway in the building.

The front hall in both directions was empty. He took the key ring out of his pocket. He was searching for the one that would open the office door when the clang of something metal and the crunch of paper stopped him.

Swearing silently, he stuffed the keys back in his pocket, walked casually a few feet down the hall and then furtively peered around a corner. The door to the director's office was slightly open and light was spilling out into the hall.

Curtis pulled back out of sight, his ears straining to catch every sound. He waited. The door closed. If the cleaning woman was moving this way toward the personnel office, his chance to get in the office unseen would be gone. Curtis held his breath, prepared to put a smile on his face if she came around the corner and met him face-to-face. Shuffling footsteps grew faint, retreating down the hall.

Quickly Curtis walked back to the door of the business office. He found the right key, and in one quick movement, he unlocked the door and slipped inside. Leaning against the door for a moment, he allowed his eyes to adjust to the sudden darkness. One small desk lamp had been left on, but the small circle of light did little to dispel the cavernous darkness stretching back from the front counter to a row of desks, computers and filing cabinets.

Curtis took out a pocket flashlight and let it play over the drawers of the cabinets as he passed them. When he found one that promised the files he wanted, he searched Myra's key ring. At first, he thought there wasn't a key small enough to fit the tiny lock but he patiently tried them all a second time and discovered that he had just missed the right one in the dim light.

Curtis pulled the top drawer open, searched through the folders until he found the ones that he wanted. Ignoring the chair next to the desk lamp, he sat down on the floor, out of sight from anyone who might glance in the office but bathed in the light from the lamp. He began taking notes from each personnel folder as he carefully reviewed all the contents. He was methodical in his search and felt more than one pang of guilt as he read several reports marked Confidential.

His interest centered on the annual physical examination required of every employee, and on the names and addresses listed under personal background information. If he had expected something dramatic to leap out at him, he was disappointed. Even though he'd found some items of interest in the files, he wouldn't know if they were pertinent without a lot more follow-up.

He put the files back and furtively locked the office door after him. Back in his own office, he spread out his notes, marking some with question marks. He entertained both a feeling of hopelessness and expectancy. He had a gut feeling that the missing answer was there—if he could just find it.

Chapter Sixteen

Curtis took all his notes home with him. He didn't want to take a chance of Myra's finding them in his desk. The next morning he called the office as soon as he thought his secretary was in.

"I'm going to be in the field this morning, Myra," he told her. "I should finish up by eleven. Can we hold all my appointments until then?"

There was a puzzled pause. "I thought we'd caught up on all your outside interviews."

Curtis swore under his breath. That was the trouble with having a competent secretary. She recognized a thin alibi when she heard one.

"Is it Gail Richards again?" she demanded in a caustic tone. "You've spent more time on that one client than a dozen others combined. Don't you think that woman's demands on a rehab counselor are a little bit on the ridiculous side? I mean, really, Curtis, people are beginning to talk. I've tried to explain—"

"I know I can depend on you to set them straight, Myra," Curtis said dryly.

"It's not easy...not with you taking her home every afternoon. It looks...well, it looks as though you're personally interested in her." There was a questioning lift to her voice.

Curtis was not going to deny the truth...nor was he going to verify it for a bunch of gossipy women. He briskly changed the subject, asking Myra to collect some figures for a federal report that had to be made each month. "We can work on it when I get back to the office. Bye." He flinched a little when she hung up the receiver with a definite slam.

IN READING Roberta Benson's file, he had found two things of interest: first, the physical therapist had filed for personal bankruptcy this past year; and second, a social worker's report indicated that Roberta was financially responsible for a child who had been committed to the Stratford Institution for disabled children. It was the word *child* that had brought Curtis to the institution. Lamont had said that the assailant's psychological profile indicated maternal frustration. The police had all kinds of investigative machinery at their disposal, but some facets of an investigation couldn't be handled that way. Not human emotions...not hunches...not imperceptible personality changes. In his profession he dealt as much in the subjective aspects of life as in the objective.

A small group of children in a fenced enclosure were yelling and squealing as they played under the supervision of three attendants. A couple of friendly kids grinned and waved at Curtis as he went past. Inside the building, two women worked at desks behind a long counter. Both of them were young. Both of them chewed gum. When one looked up and saw Curtis, her mouth stopped in the middle of a chew. She stood up, gave her hair a pat and came quickly over to the counter.

"May I help you?"

Curtis gave her a slow smile. "I'm sure you can."

The girl flushed and Curtis felt a little guilty for his flirtatious approach. He handed her his business card.

She smiled. "Yes, Mr. O'Mallory?"

"A situation has come to our attention that indicates my office might be of help to one of our therapists," he lied. "I'd appreciate knowing if Roberta Benson needs any assistance in meeting her financial obligation. I understand she's responsible for one of the children here."

The girl clicked her gum and nodded, "That's right. Her sister."

Not her own child. Curtis had been expecting a different relationship. "Her sister?"

"That's right. Maribelle's thirteen or fourteen years, I guess. Anyway, the payments have been worked out."

"Was Maribelle injured in a car accident, by any chance?"

"Nope. Birth defect. Severe cerebral palsy. Been here since she was born."

"Does her sister, Roberta Benson, come to see her Maribelle often? Are they close? I mean, does Roberta seem extremely attached to her sister?"

The girl thought for a moment and then shook her head. "Miss Benson pays the bills and that's about it. She doesn't come around like a lot of families do— maybe because Maribelle doesn't remember anybody.

She's not real lovable, if you know what I mean. You can't blame the sister. She has her own life to live.'' The girl gave a philosophical click of her gum.

Curtis thanked her for her time. On the drive back to the office, he went over the information he'd gained and found absolutely nothing in it to indicate Roberta was suffering from maternal frustration.

There was a disappointed slump to his shoulders as he went in his office. Myra looked up from her desk, her blue eyes giving him a measured scrutiny that would have made him uncomfortable under different circumstances. ''You're back early.''

He nodded. ''I was trying to assist... another counselor, but it didn't work out. Well, what's on for today?''

She told him and he shook his head. ''I don't see how we're going to get on the top of everything— without putting in some extra time.'' He thought a minute. ''I hate to ask, but would you mind if I dropped by your place for a couple of hours tonight?''

The way her eyes lit up made him feel like a cad. ''Not at all. Why don't we order in pizza or something, and get an early start.''

''Sounds good.'' He started toward his inner office but she stopped him.

''Curtis, I think someone was in my desk last night. One of the drawers wasn't completely closed this morning. Several things were slightly out of place... like my keys. I was wondering if I ought to report it.''

He kept his expression bland. ''Anything missing?''

"Not that I can tell."

"Well, it was probably one of the cleaning ladies snooping around for something to eat." He grinned at her. "You don't have dark secrets hidden in there, have you?"

The question was at odds with a notation on Myra's physical record. She'd had an abortion fifteen months ago, a year after her divorce and the trauma of losing the custody of her son.

CURTIS WASN'T ABLE to get away from the office that afternoon until Gail was almost ready to leave.

"I thought you'd forgotten me," she chided as they walked out to his car, his arm possessively through hers.

"Paperwork. My caseload is over a hundred now and there must be a dozen forms every week on each client."

"I feel guilty taking up so much of your time."

Curtis was about to respond when Myra came up behind them on the narrow sidewalk. She brushed by on Curtis's side, turned around and took a few steps backward as she faced him. She ignored Gail completely.

"I forgot to ask...what time do you want supper?" Her tone was intimate and her smile splashed over him.

Curtis felt Gail's arm tighten under his. He swore silently, but there wasn't anything he could do but say, "How about seven?"

"Great. See you then." She gave him a wink and crossed the parking lot to her bright red Le Baron.

Curtis and Gail walked in silence the rest of the way to his car. As he closed her door and walked around to the driver's side, he knew he had to say something, but what? He didn't want to tell Gail the truth—that he had set up the date with Myra so he could play detective. If he launched into a defensive explanation, she might get the wrong idea completely.

In the end, he simply said, "Myra and I have to work tonight." He felt like a little boy trying to make up a story.

"I see." Her eyes were round and innocent. "Homework?"

When he caught a hint of a smile on the corner of her lips, he laughed. "Perfectly innocent, I assure you." She'd deftly backed him into a corner. The work excuse didn't wash.

Her expression was patient, waiting.

"All right, I'm going there under false pretenses . . . but I swear it's for strictly nonromantic reasons." He leaned toward her and tipped her chin gently as he kissed her. "And I'll be thinking about you every minute, I promise."

Myra saw their embrace as she drove past and her red lips tightened. Then she relaxed and smiled. Curtis wanted to spend some time with her. The lame excuse of needing to catch up on work was just that—a lame excuse.

She lived in an eastern suburb of Denver in a small tract house. Curtis suspected that the developer had gone bankrupt before the development was complete. Myra's home was the only one on her side of the street, even though improvements had been made for more additional houses. Curtis had picked up his secretary several times for conferences and business meetings but he'd never been inside her house.

She answered the doorbell promptly. "Come on in . . . you're right on time."

The front door opened into a small living room, and he was surprised that it was filled with cheap furnishings. Not at all what one would imagine a sharp dresser like Myra to choose, thought Curtis.

As if reading his mind, she said flatly, "My husband got all the good stuff. I decided I could either spend money on the house, or on myself, and I won."

"Good choice," he said, sitting down on a faded tweed couch.

She was wearing a casual midnight blue jumpsuit made of a soft material that clung to her in all the right places. Pearl earrings matched a gold chain pendant. Curtis suspected that she'd gone to the beauty shop after work because her hair glinted with a new auburn rinse. Her appearance made a statement all right, thought Curtis. *A determined woman on the prowl.*

"The pizza should be here shortly. Beer?"

"Great."

She brought in a couple of foaming mugs, set them on the coffee table and then eased down beside him on the couch. Her perfume was a cloying scent. And if he hadn't known her so well, he might have mistaken her feminine purring as evidence of a gentle nature, but he knew better. She had a core as hard as flint.

"It must be lonely for you living alone...especially after you've once had a family," he said, smiling, hoping the comment didn't sound as abrupt to her as it did to him. The way she was spinning her feminine web, he wanted to make his stay as short as possible.

She looked over the rim of her mug and smiled. "I have plenty of company...when I want it."

"Does your son ever get to come for a visit?"

Her blue eyes darkened. "No." Then she shrugged. "He lives in Vermont...with his father and his grandparents."

"It's unusual for a father to get full custody... especially of a young child. How old is he now?"

"Five. He was two when...when the court took him from me."

"Why?"

Her painted lips stiffened slightly. "Drugs. I got in with some heavy users. Country-club swingers, you know. Plenty of parties, admiring men, wonderful food and dishes of cocaine passed around for dessert. My husband wasn't a part of the scene...so he divorced me, convinced the court that I was an unfit mother." She gave Curtis a brittle smile. "So here I am. Straight and drinking beer with my boss. How's that for a gay divorcée?"

"I admire you for getting your life back together—"

"Oh, get off the counselor crap." She set her mug down on the coffee table with a bang. "Save it for Gail Richards. She's better at acting all hurt and innocent than I am. If I killed some kid with my car, everyone would be on my neck. But that broad has everyone fooled," she flashed angrily. "Including you, dear boss."

"And you think she should be punished?" he asked evenly.

Red coals burned hotly in her eyes. "I paid for my mistakes! Why shouldn't she pay for hers?"

Like gates on a spillover suddenly opened, the rush of festering rancor from Myra's lips was like nothing Curtis had ever experienced. Foul, vindictive hate spewed from her and revealed a tortured soul that was bent on revenge for what life had done to her.

He listened to the ugly story of a pretty young wife turned by drugs into a junkie and social prostitute. In the end, she lost everything...her home, husband and child.

"I got straight...and then I met Paul on the rebound. He promised me a home and children." Something hard crept into her eyes. "But I got pregnant...and *then* he told me he was happily married."

Curtis watched her finish her beer in one gulp. "So I got an abortion. Want another beer?" she asked in the same tone of voice. She went in the kitchen and brought back two more bottles.

"That must have been rough," Curtis said evenly.

She shrugged. "As I said before, I've paid for my mistakes." Then she gave him a brittle smile. "But enough of that. You get plenty of emotional garbage dumped on you on the job. Time you relaxed and enjoyed yourself." The invitation was blatant, matched by the way she put one arm on the back of the cushion and let one finger lightly play with the hair on the back of his head.

He gave a self-mocking chuckle. "I'm not the relaxing kind, I'm afraid. You know that, Myra."

"People change."

"I'm not sure they do, not way down deep." He
leaned forward and made a pretense of filling his mug,
which was still half-full. He was glad the way the conversation was going. He was getting an insight to
Myra's troubled personality. "I suspect that you still
would like a husband and family."

"Oh, come off it, Curtis. Let's don't play games.
I've come to terms with who I am." Her laugh was
brittle again. "No more lying to myself or pretending
that I need to find my one and only. Save all that crap
for some ninny like Richards."

"You don't like her, do you?"

"Shows, does it?"

"Any special reason?"

"No...just on general principles...and maybe she
reminds me of the woman who broke up my marriage." Myra seemed to struggle for something light to
say, even as her eyes remained cold, resentful. She put
a possessive hand on Curtis's arm. "You and I understand each other. No strings...no commitments...
just a couple of people who know how to enjoy themselves."

"Is that how you see me, Myra?"

A wash of different emotions swept across her face.
Then her lower lip quivered. "No. I see you as someone I can never have."

GAIL HAD ACCEPTED an invitation to have dinner with
Angie and Tony at their home after asking Sergeant

Rossini if it would be all right. The officer took one look at Tony's brawny, muscular frame and decided that Gail was in good protective hands.

"When you get ready to bring her home," Rossini instructed Tony, "call me at the precinct and I'll be back at the house by the time you get here."

Tony nodded. "I'll deliver her home safely—you can depend on that, Officer."

Gail was grateful for the outing. It gave her something to think about besides Curtis spending the evening with his attractive secretary. On the surface she had behaved very adult about the situation, but her calm acceptance had not gone very deep. In fact, she had been shaken more than she cared to admit to anyone—even herself.

When she told Angie that Curtis was working late at Myra's house, Angie didn't mince words about what she thought about Gail's guarded acceptance of Curtis's attentions.

"It's that damn infuriating pride of yours. Good grief, gal, don't you think a guy like that knows the difference between love and pity? Sure, Curtis is damn sorry about what's been happening to you—we all are—but wake up, Gail. Where'd you get the idea that you had to be one-hundred-percent perfect for someone to fall in love with you?"

"It's just that—"

"That you're afraid to trust him."

"I am not! He's the most trustworthy, dependable man I've ever met."

Angie smiled at her bristling indignation. "Then if the man says he loves you—believe him!"

CURTIS LEFT Myra's house without eating the pizza or opening his briefcase. As he drove back to his apartment, his feelings were contradictory. In some ways, Myra fit the profile Lamont had offered. She certainly had reasons to be maternally frustrated—she'd lost the custody of one child and aborted another. Suppressed anger might cause her to lash out in some twisted way. Her animosity toward Gail was certainly plain enough. There was nothing to connect her with Wilhite except that he'd been at Crestview briefly. As far as Curtis had been able to learn, Myra didn't even know Sherrie Sinclair. On the plus side, he'd gained an insight into his secretary that he hadn't had before, but the bottom line was that he had failed to come up with any leads that might provide the evidence he had gone after.

He called Gail's house as soon as he returned to his apartment, but her telephone recording message was on. She'd left a number where she could be reached. Puzzled, he dialed it and was relieved to hear Angie's robust hello.

As soon as he identified himself, Angie assured him Gail was there and invited him to join them. "We're just finishing up dinner...and about to have dessert...apple pie à la mode. Got a nice big piece with your name on it."

His empty stomach rumbled appreciatively at the thought. Myra's pizza had gone unnoticed. He wrote down the address. "Are you sure it's all right with Gail?"

"Positive. She'll be delighted."

He was there in about twenty minutes. "You look ready for the slopes," Angie chided as she took his coat and scarf.

He laughed. "Radio says a storm's coming...new powder expected at Beaver Run." He pushed back a strand of silvered hair as he turned and smiled at Gail. "Hi. Fancy meeting you here."

He sat down beside her, and the room was suddenly filled with a breathless energy. Gail's voice was a little shaky as she said, "You got through early."

He nodded but didn't elaborate. A deepening of lines around his eyes suggested an inner tension, and she wondered what had happened to the "work" session. When Angie offered him some leftover chicken and dumplings, he readily accepted and Gail knew he hadn't eaten.

They gathered around a round oak table in the dining room. "My grandfather was a furniture maker of the old country," Tony said with pride, pointing out a beautiful hand-carved buffet. Angie entertained them with a story about Tony's grandpa's making rocking chairs that he sold on the sidewalks of New York before he could afford a shop.

Curtis showed his interest in "people" stories and kept them talking about their families while he demonstrated his appreciation for Angie's cooking by accepting second helpings. It was the first time Gail had seen Curtis in a family setting, and she smiled when he and Tony got involved in a heated exchange about the Denver Broncos.

Angie raised her eyes and said, "Men."

The evening passed quickly as the four of them sat around the table eating pie and enjoying a comfortable companionship. Reluctantly Gail decided it was time to go.

Tony called Sergeant Rossini at the police station. "We're on our way." Then he put on his hat and coat.

"I can see Gail home," protested Curtis.

"Okay," Tony answered readily. "But I'll follow in my car," he added with a stubborn jut to his chin. "I told Rossini I'd be responsible. That means making sure Gail gets back to the house safe and sound."

"Tony...maybe they don't want a chaperon," chided Angie as she handed Gail her pale blue car coat and helped her loop a multicolored winter scarf under her chin.

"Tough." Tony gave Curtis a knowing grin. "Sorry, bud, but we *both* see the lady home."

Angie teased Gail as they left. "Some women aren't content with *one* handsome man."

CURTIS WAS clearly irritated as he glanced in the mirror and saw the reflection of Tony's headlights all the way across Denver. Gail knew he was growling under his breath and she laughed silently. Her spirits were higher than they had been for a long time. The warmth and companionship of the evening had relaxed her. She was pleased that her good friends had accepted Curtis without reservation.

Angie's smiling glances had been the kind that said, See! I told you. He's in love with you.

Gail sighed happily as she snuggled close to him in the front seat. For the first time, she dared to believe that she'd found a man she could love with all her heart.

"Nice people...Angie and Tony," he said, taking a curve at a deliberate speed to throw her nicely against him. She didn't pull back or object when he put his arm around her and drove with one hand.

"Very nice," she murmured happily. She was enveloped in a warm cocoon, content and safe. The knowledge that he had come to Angie's tonight because he wanted to be with her mocked her uneasiness about his date with Myra. She didn't know what had happened to his plans to spend the evening with his secretary, but she had seen tension in his face when he had first come in the house. Whatever had happened, he wasn't talking about it, and she was glad. She didn't want Myra or anyone else to intrude on the happiness that the evening had brought.

"Aren't you driving awfully slow," she chided, noticing the speedometer only registering forty in a fifty-five speed zone. She'd bet Tony was chewing nails at the snail's pace.

Curtis grinned. "Serves him right."

When they reached her house, the sergeant's car was parked at the far end of the driveway.

"Well, I guess we trade one chaperon for another," Curtis muttered as he pulled in the driveway and parked at the side porch steps. Then he turned to Gail. "But before we do—"

She welcomed his hungry kisses. Her fingers threaded through the beautiful waves of salt-and-pepper hair as an incredible surge of desire ran rampant through her body. All of the defenses she had built against him melted like wax in a fiery flame. Out of all the pain and darkness, a miracle had made her shattered life whole and wonderful. *Love you... love you... love you.* The phrase filled her mind like a melody in perfect accompaniment to his kisses and caresses.

When Tony tapped on the windowpane, they ignored his presence as long as they could. ''Can't you order him off the property... or have him arrested as a nuisance?''

Gail gave a breathless chuckle. ''He's not going to go... until I'm safely inside.''

''Blast it all! You're safe with me.''

''He's not going to go away.'' She unlocked her car door. Tony promptly opened it and offered a hand to help her out. ''Sorry, lovebirds, but it's darn cold standing out here.''

''You could leave!'' snapped Curtis.

''A promise is a promise.''

As the three of them mounted the side steps together, Gail was pinned in the middle between the two men. She was glad that she'd quit using her cane a couple of days ago because it felt wonderful to loop her arms through theirs.

Curtis unlocked the door and then bowed at Tony as he held the door for Gail to enter the vestibule. ''Your mission has been accomplished. The lady is safely delivered home.''

Tony hesitated.

''Get lost,'' Curtis ordered. ''Sergeant Rossini is standing in the hall watching through the glass doors. Enough is enough!''

Tony chuckled. "No need to get testy, man." Then he gave Gail's shoulders a clumsy squeeze and kissed her cheek. "Take care."

"Thanks, Tony, for a wonderful evening."

His glance took in her flushed cheeks. "Sure," he said with a grin. They could hear him chuckling as he closed the outer door.

Curtis pulled Gail into his arms again. She kissed him as fervently as before, not caring what the policewoman thought. She was getting used to living in a goldfish bowl. Curtis didn't seem to mind, either, and when he finally pulled away, his voice was husky. "I think I'd better go...."

"You could come in for a nightcap."

"I'm tempted but..." His gaze swept lovingly over her face. "You need your rest." He took one of her hands and placed a kiss in the middle of her palm, then closed up the fingers. "Save it until you're in bed...a good-night kiss." He held the glass door open for her. "Sweet dreams, my love." Then he quickly went out the front door as if he were afraid his self-control would run out.

Sergeant Rossini wasn't in the hall, but Gail could hear the teakettle whistling. The policewoman liked strong tea to keep her alert through the night. Remembering Curtis's passionate kiss, Gail was glad the officer had let them have a few minutes of privacy.

Gail seemed to float down the hall when in fact her steps were slow but steady even without her cane. She felt a rush of thankfulness that her body had responded to the vigorous exercises and she was getting strong enough to move about without being in danger of losing her balance.

As she entered the kitchen, the teakettle was sending puffs of steam into the air. A cup and saucer had been placed on the table, but there was no sign of the policewoman. Probably down the hall using my bathroom, thought Gail, crossing the kitchen to turn off a glowing red burner. Careless of her to leave—

The rest of the thought was cut off. She felt rather than saw a movement from the direction of the butler's pantry. Before she could swing around, arms like a tightening vise went around her.

A moist cloth went over her nose and mouth, choking off the air and filling her nostrils with a sickening sweet smell. Spots of light like firecrackers began to explode in her head. Instant nausea sent bile up into her throat. Her legs and arms floated away from her.

The shrill whistle of the teakettle faded away as a stab of a needle in her arm obliterated all sensation. She felt herself going down, down, sucked into a dark abyss.

Chapter Seventeen

When Gail came back to consciousness, she was lying on the floor, still wearing her blue coat. Opening her heavy-lidded eyes, she squinted with blurry vision up at the bars of a cage. She moved her head and all shapes and colors of animals stared down at her with glassy eyes. Their heads and ears and bodies swirled in a macabre dance as they grew into monstrous proportions or shrank into pinpoints of light. Her head whirled sickeningly, sending bitter bile up into her dry mouth. Even as darkness closed over again, she whimpered.

The next time she came back to consciousness, she didn't open her eyes but lay motionless with her cheek pressed against the hardness of floorboards. The whirling inside her skull stopped but pain like jagged shards of glass stabbed at her closed eyes. She was afraid to move, fearful that her head would split apart. A vaporous darkness claimed her again and once more she floated off into a fitful sleep.

The next time she awoke, the pain in her head had eased. Hazy thoughts began to penetrate her consciousness. Fragmented memories began to form. As

memory rushed back, so did raw fear. Her eyes flew
open. There was sunlight now but muted and soft. She
moved her head cautiously, blinking as she struggled
to focus her eyes. The bars of the cage were still there.
No, not a cage. A baby crib. She could see the animals clearly now. All kinds, all colors, dozens of
stuffed animals lining a long shelf above the baby bed.

Gail struggled to sit up. She leaned against the wall
for support, wincing from the pain in her head. A
musty, dusty smell filled her nostrils and her eyes
widened with disbelief as she looked around the room.

Like a shrine, toys, baby clothes and infant para-
phernalia filled every wall and corner. Unopened bottles of baby lotion, oil and diapers lined the dusty
shelves. Magazine pictures of babies and samplers of
nursery rhymes covered the walls. Gail's skin crawled.
Everything in the room was new—and unused.

The faint sound of a door closing somewhere in the
house sounded as if it came from a floor below. She
was on the second floor of a house. Whose house?

The one who wants you dead.

Gail's mind handled the truth with a strange de-
tachment. A weird kind of relief came with the
knowledge that the diabolical game was almost played
out. Her tormenter had made her move. The harassment was over. No more searching the shadows for the
hidden face. Soon she would know. She stared at the
door and pictured it opening. Would her life be over
when her tormenter stood there?

Biting her lip and using every ounce of strength she
could muster, Gail pulled herself to her feet using the
bars of the crib. As she stood beside it, she wavered

unsteadily. She clutched the top bar for support until her dizziness eased. Holding the crib railing, she moved around the bed until she could reach out and touch the nearest piece of furniture, which was a white chest of drawers covered with Peter Rabbit decals. Like a child trying its first steps, she didn't trust herself to walk without touching something for support. Cautiously she edged toward the door as she reached out and touched another chest and then a chair. *Hurry. Hurry.*

She reached the last piece of furniture between her and the door, which was a cartlike stand for changing diapers, a flat top and drawers underneath. Gail looked at the distance from it to the closed door, and despair caught in her throat. *I can't do it.* She'd only been walking a couple of days without a cane, and in her present drugged state, her muscles were less dependable than ever. She didn't have the balance to let loose of the supporting cart and walk across the floor on her own. She leaned heavily against the infant stand and felt it move slightly under the pressure.

It was on rollers!

Testing it, she gave it another little push . . . and another . . . and another. Holding on to it for balance, she moved it slowly forward toward the door, taking small steps beside it. To her own ears, the cart seemed to move silently, but she couldn't be sure. She feared that someone on the floor below might easily hear the movement.

When the doorknob was within reach, she leaned forward and turned the blackened brass knob. *Please, God, don't let it be locked.* Her prayer was answered.

She slowly opened the door all the way and stood for a long minute staring out into a short hall. Light from below flowed up an old staircase, revealing a worn rug, a high shadowy ceiling and two other doors, both closed.

Gail held her breath, eyed the railing at the top of the stairs and firmed her courage. An able-bodied person could have covered the distance in a half-dozen steps, but to Gail it was like looking through the wrong end of a telescope. Her head was light and waves of dizziness continued to make her balance unsteady. She hung over the cart, clinging to it as her legs threatened to buckle under her. She knew that it would be insanity to try to walk the distance without the support of the changing table. Slow as her progress would be, she had no choice but to take minuscule steps beside the cart as she pushed it down the short hall. Once she got to the stairs, she could grab hold of the banister and ease down the steps one at a time. Thank heavens, she'd been going up and down her own stairs, albeit with help. If she could make it to the front door and outside—

The floorboards squeaked and the rolling wheels sounded louder as she inched toward the top step. The muffled sounds of a TV or radio floated up from below, no doubt responsible for her movements going unnoticed, she thought gratefully. Her steps grew more firm, and when she reached the top of the stairs, a sense of victory was there. She looked down and saw that the front door was only a foot from the bottom step.

Easy now, she warned herself as she transferred her hold from the cart to the railing. Holding on to the banister with both hands, she eased her right foot down to the first step and then cautiously followed it with the other one. In this fashion, she had descended about five steps. Then her left leg gave way.

One minute she was upright, the next off balance, standing on one leg.

She clung to the banister, trying to recover as she shifted her weight to the other leg. The right leg refused to take extra strain. It buckled.

Gail fell forward, her hands flailing the air as she lost her grip on the banister. Her body made a half twist as she fell forward. Her last thought was her doctor's warning her not to fall. Her forehead struck the edge of a step in the downward slide. Pain exploded in her head—and then nothing.

WHEN SERGEANT ROSSINI didn't make her twelve o'clock check-in call, and didn't answer the phone when the dispatcher rang, officers Kline and Mantelli were sent immediately to check it out.

They found the front door locked. When Sergeant Rossini didn't answer the doorbell, the two officers exchanged wordless glances. They drew their guns and cautiously made their way around the house to the back door. They found it ajar.

Mantelli covered his partner as he eased inside. Muffled sounds came from the butler's pantry. The two officers positioned themselves on each side of the door. Kline nodded at Mantelli, gave the door a kick. As it flew open, they leveled their guns ready to fire. Sergeant Rossini lay on the floor, gagged and bound with clothesline. The smell of chloroform was heavy in the air. Her eyes were heavy as they focused gratefully on the two policemen. She told them that she'd been at the stove, preparing hot water for tea when someone jumped her from behind, slapping a cloth reeking of chloroform over her nose and mouth. "When I came to...I was tied up. I kicked the cupboard, hoping someone would hear."

"Where's Miss Richards? Is she in the house?"

"I don't know. She wasn't here when I got here...but she could have come while I was knocked out."

"Stay here. We'll check it out."

Left alone in the kitchen, the policewoman sat at the table and rested her head in her hand. There'd be hell to pay for this.

Lieutenant Lamont made Officer Rossini's worst fears a reality. He snapped questions with rapidity of a repeating revolver. "What in the hell happened? Where's Miss Richards? Why wasn't the damn place secured?"

She tried to explain, but he jumped on her every word.

"You're too busy making tea to tend to your job, is that it? You went on duty at six o'clock and yet you didn't arrive at the house until nearly nine-thirty?"

Rossini straightened her shoulders. "Miss Richards was having dinner across town with friends...."

"And you took the time off instead of doing your duty and going with her."

"I *didn't* take the time off...and she was in the company of a muscular bruiser who was protection enough. I was working on reports when Mr. Difalco called me at the precinct and told me he was bringing her home. I came straight here. The front door was locked...."

"And the back?"

She paled. "I didn't check it right away... I would have made the rounds shortly, so..."

"So you decided to have a cup of tea first," Lamont finished caustically.

She nodded.

"How long were you in the house?"

"Just a few minutes."

"So someone must have already been here when you came in?"

She nodded wearily. "Must have been... in the pantry, waiting."

"And you never heard Miss Richards come back."

"No... I thought I'd take my tea into the sitting room and wait for her."

Lamont snapped an order to one of his men. "Call the Difalco residence. Find out if Miss Richards is still there... if not, find out what time she left. If Mr. Difalco brought her home, tell him she's missing and I want him over here right away for questioning."

"WHAT?" Curtis barked into the phone.

"Gail...she's not home." Angie's tone was strained, then she asked in a more hopeful tone. "Is she with you?"

"No, she's not with me. What do you mean she's not at home?" He felt his chest tighten. "I left her there a couple of hours ago."

"The police just called . . . wanting to know if Gail was still here. When Tony said he'd seen her home sometime after ten o'clock, the officer told him he was needed to answer some questions. They wouldn't tell him anything." She swallowed by a sob. "You don't think something terrible has happened to her, do you?" Angie sobbed. "She was so happy tonight. I can't believe anyone would want to harm her. It must be a mistake . . . a terrible mistake. She's safe and sound. . . ." But Angie's watery voice was at odds with the hopeful words.

Curtis hung up the phone, threw on his clothes and was out the door as if the place were on fire. His thoughts echoed Angie's disbelief. How could Gail be missing? She had been safely inside the house when he left her and the policewoman's car had been in the driveway. Otherwise, he and Tony would have waited for the officer. He remembered that he had heard the whistle of a teakettle when he let Gail into the hall.

He beat Tony to the house because the distance was shorter. Policemen were swarming over the house and grounds. Almost every window was ablaze with lights. The contrast to the quiet serenity when he had kissed Gail good-night was a physical shock.

Lamont glared at him, openly irritated answering Curtis's barrage of questions until Curtis told him that he had brought Gail home.

"I thought Mr. Difalco did?" countered the lieutenant.

"We both did. Tony followed in his car and Gail rode with me."

"And you both came inside—"

"No, Tony just saw us to the door. He waited until I unlocked it and guided Gail inside. Then he left. We...Gail and I said good-night in the vestibule. Not that we had that much privacy. Sergeant Rossini was watching through the glass doors, waiting for Gail to come in."

"Sergeant Rossini was there, tonight, watching?"

Curtis frowned. "I assumed she was...."

"But you didn't actually see her?"

Curtis thought back. He remembered telling Tony about the officer being a chaperon, but he wasn't sure it was because he'd glimpsed her standing in the hall. "She always waited for Gail." He felt a sickening twist in his stomach.

"Did you see the officer or not?"

"I—I guess I just assumed..." Curtis went pale. "You mean I left Gail here and the officer was already knocked out?"

"Looks that way. Miss Richards must have walked into the kitchen and was attacked the same way as the officer. She says someone was hiding in the butler's pantry and subdued her with chloroform before tying her up." His eyes narrowed. "Only the second time, the victim wasn't left behind. My men found this in the alley." He held out Gail's multicolored scarf. "Recognize it?"

Curtis's mouth was dry. "It's Gail's."

"Was she wearing it tonight?"

He nodded. "With a pale blue car coat." He remembered how lovely she had looked in a harmonizing soft blouse that made her eyes deep pools of blue green. His chest tightened and for a moment he couldn't speak.

"And—" prodded Lamont impatiently.

Curtis steeled himself and described the blouse as best he could. "Blue slacks and black suede boots... knee-high."

"We found evidence of a car recently parked in the back alley," said Lamont. "She must have been taken out that way. I've got officers going up and down the block, asking if anyone saw a car parked there. Sometimes we get lucky. Maybe somebody putting out garbage noticed something."

He touched Curtis's arm. "That's what detective work amounts to—turning over small stones and hoping to find something underneath."

He told Lamont about his session with Myra earlier that evening. "I thought maybe I could get some insight that would be helpful. She could have come here after I left her house and went across town to the Difalcos'."

"I'll send a car out to her place." He didn't sound optimistic.

Every minute that passed brought a growing fear stabbing Curtis's insides like a knife. *They had to find her before—* His mind blocked the rest of it.

"Go home, Curtis," Lamont ordered. "There's nothing you can do here. I'll call if there's any development."

WORRY, EXHAUSTION and raw fear wired Curtis for an explosion as he waited through the long night beside his phone. The inactivity was pure torture. He wanted to be doing something—but what? His mind wrestled with the tangled mesh of Larry's death, Scuffy's assault and Gail's abduction. He was more convinced than ever that all the incidents were bound together. But how?

Chapter Eighteen

Gail woke up on the floor, lying in the same corner where she had been before. This time her hands and her feet were tied to the legs of the crib and she lay on her side facing the baby bed. Blood from a cut and bump on her forehead had dripped onto the floor and congealed on her cheek. Her body seemed to be a collection of disjointed hurting pieces. As she slipped in and out of consciousness, her thoughts were like vaporous shadows, refusing to form themselves with any clarity. She had a vague memory of inching her way to the head of the stairs but before she could capture it, the impression faded.

She slipped back into a fitful sleep and when she awoke the sunlight was less bright through lacy Priscilla curtains, and she could see light snow falling against a leaden sky. For a moment Gail lay mesmerized by the whirl of snowflakes, light and fanciful as they collected on the outside sill.

She felt the movement of the rocking chair before she heard its squeak. She was no longer alone in the room. The crib blocked her vision, but as she lay with her cheek pressed against the floor, she could see under it. With great effort, Gail focused her eyes on wooden rockers moving in rhythm to the gentle push of a pair of brown boots. Back and forth, back and forth. The motion was mesmerizing, and Gail stared mindlessly. Her senses were dulled and a drugged inertia kept her passive. Over the squeak of the chair, Gail heard a woman's soft voice crooning, "Tur-ra-lura-lura...hush now don't you cry. Tur-ra-lura-li...that's an Irish lullaby."

Slowly the simple lyrics became cold fingers twisting Gail's insides. She closed her eyes. *This isn't happening. It's a nightmare.*

The chair suddenly stopped squeaking. Gail's eyes flew open. She watched the brown boots move closer and closer. Then she could see the woman on the other side of the crib as she lowered a baby doll gently down in the bed and covered it with a blue blanket.

"Sleep tight," she said softly, her hair falling forward over her cheeks.

As she raised up, she looked into the corner and her eyes met Gail's. "Oh, so you're awake," she said in a bright tone of satisfaction.

ON SATURDAY, only nursing personnel were on duty at Crestview. The offices were closed and no therapy sessions were offered. Most of the parking lot was empty as Curtis pulled into his parking place. A light snow was falling, and the radio reported that the high country had already received several inches.

Curtis sat down at his desk and called Lamont. The dispatcher informed him that the detective was out. "Any message?"

"Yes, ask him to call this number when he comes in."

Please, please find her. The words were a silent cry. He hung up and for a moment such anguish poured over him. Pain attacked his whole body. He had brought Gail home nearly twelve hours ago. *Where is she? Is she still alive?* His mind refused to handle the most tormenting question of all—was it already too late?

After a moment, he raised his head. Gail was the most courageous woman he had ever met. He knew she would fight to her last breath. Just thinking of her strength steeled his determination to do the same. He had every confidence that Lamont would handle the investigation with dispatch, but he also knew that the wheels of bureaucracy grind slowly—sometimes too slowly to prevent the next crime. The police would be questioning Myra and getting alibis from people like Roberta Benson, Inga Neilson and Edith Crum.

Curtis opened his briefcase and took out the material he had copied from the personnel files. Deep in his gut, he felt that some vital fact was in these records if he could only find it. Reaching for the phone, he began calling the names that had been listed as next of kin, and people given as references for Myra, Roberta, the pretty nurse, Ellyn, Beth and the head nurse, Mabel Tewsberry, who had a running feud with both Larry and Scuffy. Somebody held the information that would bring the picture into focus. He prayed he would recognize the missing piece when it turned up.

GAIL LOOKED UP into the woman's face and read the raw message in her eyes. *My pain will be gone when you are dead.*

"You," whispered Gail.

"Yes, me," Beth Scott said, smiling.

"I never once..."

"I know. You made everything so easy. The way you left your purse lying around during therapy, I could easily make an impression of your house key. I was afraid you might keep changing your locks and leave your key ring at home—but you never did." She gave a happy laugh. "Recognize this? I found it in the attic." She moved a cradle so Gail could see it. "It was all scratched and ugly, but I sanded it all down.... Nice finish, don't you think? The eyelet ruffles add a softness to it. Very soothing for a baby." She rocked the empty cradle lovingly. Her smile was faraway and misty.

Gail was stunned. All the time she'd felt someone's presence in her house, it had been Beth. From her first night home from the hospital, Beth had been the one coming in and out at will, walking around on the upper floor, leaving ugly packages and spreading filth all over the back porch. The revelation bordered on the impossible. Gail couldn't believe it. Not Beth...the healthy-looking girl who had seemed so young and wholesome, the efficient P.T. aide who had tended to her needs every day at Crestview.

"Why, Beth?" Gail asked with a thick tongue and parched mouth.

The young woman went on rocking the cradle with a glazed look in her eyes, humming softly. Her expression was vacant, like someone lost to reality. Even though her outward appearance was familiar, the young woman standing there was not the person Gail had known. Where was the therapy aide who had chatted so easily about Texas and the grandparents she loved? She must function quite normally when not suffering from a twisted reality, thought Gail. There must be a way to reason with her.

"Beth, why have you brought me here?" Gail asked in a reasonable, nonthreatening tone.

The cradle stopped abruptly. Beth looked down at Gail, and her soft expression faded. A hardness in her eyes matched her savage tone. "My baby. Somebody has to pay."

"I didn't know you had a baby, Beth. How old was he?"

"I lost Robbie even before he was born. The minute I knew I was pregnant I named him." Her lips quivered. "Don't you see, he can't rest in peace unless I show him how much I love him? There's only one way." She looked sad. "You have to die like the others."

CURTIS HAD BEEN on the phone for two hours. He had called a psychiatrist whom Myra had listed as a reference. He was surprised to find the physician in his office on Saturday.

After a couple of minutes of exchanging amenities, Curtis said, "I know that you can't divulge any privileged patient information, Doctor, but I'm helping the police with an investigation of an abduction. We have a profile on a suspect...a woman with frustrated maternal urges, probably suffering from delusions that make her lash out at people involved in car accidents where a child has been killed.''

Curtis paused and waited.

The psychiatrist cleared his throat. "Myra has been my patient for nearly two years. If you're asking me if Myra Monet fits that description, the answer is definitely no. There are no psychotic tendencies involved, I guarantee it.''

"Thank you very much.'' The disappointment in his voice must have been evident because the doctor added, ''I hope you find the one you're looking for.''

Curtis breathed an "Amen.'' He hung up and picked up the next sheet of notes. Roberta Benson. He read over the information he had found in her file, added what he learned at the Stratford home. There was absolutely nothing to indicate anything out of the ordinary, but he knew that not everything found its way into a personnel folder. Curtis dialed the number of a Miss Martha Benson whom Roberta had listed as next of kin. The address for both of them was the same.

When Curtis introduced himself, the woman said, "Oh, yes. You work at Crestview with my niece, Bobbie. She introduced us at the Christmas party." She gave a self-mocking laugh. "You probably don't remember . . . I was wearing a flowered dress with big poppies on it?''

He didn't remember the woman but he remembered the awful dress. "Yes, of course, Miss Benson. How are you? We're having a little trouble with our computer here . . . one of them in our personnel office went down," he lied, "and I volunteered to check out some of the missing information. Would you mind helping me out?"

"Not at all. Bobbie's not here. She's coaching some high school girls...she does that, you know... volunteers her time. I wish she'd quit giving so much of herself. When my brother died, Roberta's father, she had to take over the responsibility of the four younger children...and there's Maribelle, you know. Poor thing, needing care in that home."

"Must be hard on Roberta."

"A real financial strain," agreed her aunt.

"Has your niece ever consulted a psychologist or psychiatrist?"

"You mean, a shrink?" The woman gave a robust laugh that forced Curtis to hold the receiver away from his ear. "That's a good one. Bobbie's so on top of everything, it's disgusting. She's healthy, loves her work, has a dozen hobbies and has more energy than a dozen people put together."

"Has she ever had a child...or a miscarriage that you know about?" asked Curtis bluntly.

"Bobbie? Heavens, no. She's lived in my home for nearly fifteen years now. Never even had a serious relationship. Too busy." She paused as if realizing no personnel file had questions of such an intimate nature. "What is it you wanted to know?"

Curtis asked a few more benign facts, thanked her and hung up. The psychiatrist had professionally eliminated Myra, and Curtis didn't think that Roberta could get one thing past her aunt. Of course, there was always the possibility that Martha Benson was lying about her niece, but he didn't think so. Everything he'd learned about the therapist supported what he already knew about Roberta Benson.

Curtis put aside his notes on these two women. His stomach muscles contracted nervously. What was he doing sitting there making fruitless telephone calls when every minute could be a life-and-death gamble for Gail? He ran an agitated hand through his hair. What should he do? Where should he go? His thoughts raced wildly, every muscle in his body tense. He wanted to grab somebody and shake them by the throat. After a moment, he got control of himself and picked up the notes he'd made on Ellyn McPherson.

"I HAVE to go to the bathroom." Gail tried to use the same tone that Beth had responded to many times during the P.T. sessions. Day after day she had depended on Beth for all kinds of physical help. It was a gamble, but maybe habit would ease Beth into a less threatening mode. "Would you help me to the bathroom, Beth, please?" she repeated in a nonthreatening manner, as if she were lying on one of the exercise tables instead of crumpled on the floor, tied to a baby's crib.

Gail couldn't tell if Beth had even heard her. Her expression was impassive as very deliberately she set the cradle back in its place. Gail held her breath. She could see Beth's brown boots moving about on the other side of the crib.

"Beth," called Gail. "Please take me to the bathroom." She waited another agonizingly long minute

before Beth came back to her. "Thank you," Gail said
as if the request had already been granted.

With deft hands, Beth untied the knotted clothesline around Gail's wrists and ankles and helped her to
her feet. Shooting pain from cramped muscles brought
a cry from Gail's lips in spite of her effort to hold it
back. The hours she'd spent lying on the floor had
stiffened her whole body. The only good thing was
that the drugged fuzziness in her brain had lifted. Her
thinking seemed to be clear and orderly.

With one arm around Gail's waist and the other
across the front, Beth pinned Gail firmly between her
muscular arms. The old-fashioned bathroom was directly across the hall. A claw-foot tub stood in one
corner and an old silvered mirror hung above a
chipped washbasin. While Beth stood over her like a
guard dog, Gail sent a desperate look around the
room, hoping in vain to spy something that might
serve as a weapon.

Gail was afraid to say anything that might disturb
the fragile patient/aide scenario. She moistened her
dry lips and then asked if she could wash her face.
Beth nodded and, much to Gail's surprise, reached in
a cabinet for a fresh towel and washrag.

"Thank you." Gail smiled at Beth's reflection in the
mirror as the young woman stood behind her, watching every movement.

Gail was shocked by her own appearance. Her face
was bruised and bloody. A cut and bump on her forehead showed where she had struck the edge of a step
in her fall. The silk blouse she'd worn to the Difalcos'
a lifetime ago was spotted and torn. She no longer

wore the blue car coat that matched her slacks, and the silver combs she'd put in her hair were gone, leaving her hair a matted mass hanging limply around her face.

Gail kept her eyes away from her reflection as she gingerly touched the washcloth over her face, making every movement as slow as she could. Strength was flowing back into her body and her legs felt much firmer under her.

The small victory of getting Beth to do her bidding filled Gail with the hope that the woman could be manipulated if Gail were clever enough. *I have to keep things moving on a normal track until my chance comes.*

"It looks like a snowy day," Gail said pleasantly as she hung up the cloth and towel. She glanced out a window, measuring the drop from the second floor to the ground.

"A good day for a drive," Beth countered, pulling something out of the pocket of her jeans.

Gail cried out as the needle suddenly jabbed into her buttock. Beth had her pinned against the basin so she couldn't turn around. In the mirror, Gail saw her own mouth open, her eyes widen and then swirling silver and black dots distorted the reflection. Her knees bent forward. Her grasp on the edge of the sink slipped away. Darkness like a black curtain closed over her.

ELLYN MCPHERSON, the pretty brunette nurse, had listed two doctors on her medical form. Neither was available on Saturday. Their answering machines assured Curtis that his call would be brought to their notice on Monday.

Monday. He swallowed a bitter laugh and hung up. Ellyn had listed her father as next of kin and her two references were instructors at Colorado University where she had graduated five years ago. Five years! How much would former teachers know about the woman that Ellyn was today? On an impulse he rang the nurse's station on the second floor. "Is Ellyn McPherson on duty today?"

"Yes . . . but you missed her. She's on break. You'll probably find her in the cafeteria."

His first impulse was to find Ellyn and ask some direct questions, but the more he thought about it, he decided that someone who worked with her might be a better source of information.

He left his office, went upstairs where patient forms were located and wasted an hour and a half trying to find a co-worker who offered anything more decisive than the comment "Ellyn's a nice girl. A good nurse."

He had only been back in his office a few minutes, when Ellyn knocked gently on his closed door and then poked her head in. "May I come in?" Her manner was hesitant, apologetic.

"Of course, Ellyn." Curtis had mixed feelings about her sudden appearance at his office. He would have preferred to continue prying into her personal background without her knowledge.

"Is there some problem . . . about me? I mean, have I done something wrong?" Her pretty eyes were ringed with worry lines. "I heard you've been asking people questions about me. I thought . . . I thought I'd better face up to whatever it is.'' She straightened her slim shoulders even as a hint of tears hovered at the corner of her eyes.

Was she acting? Curtis decided to find out. ''Gail Richards has been kidnapped.''

A flood of emotion swept over her face that would have been beyond the most consummate actress. She steadied herself with a hand on Curtis's desk and then she dropped into a chair. ''Oh, dear Lord,'' she wailed. She fell to pieces in front of Curtis's eyes. Trembling, shaking, sobs wrenching up from her heaving chest. ''First Larry...and now Miss Richards.''

Curtis would have suffered pangs of guilt if so much hadn't been at stake. He calmed her as best he could. ''I'm asking everybody questions...trying to find something that may help the police find her before...'' He swallowed the rest. ''I'm sorry, Ellyn, but I had the idea that someone here at Crestview might be responsible for the things that have been happening.''

Her head came up. ''Like who ran over Larry?'' she blubbered. She grabbed his arm. ''I can't quit dreaming about him. I keep remembering...that wonderful warm smile of his...the confident toss of his head. It was more than just a crush...like I had on you.''

''You were in love with him,'' Curtis said softly.

She sniffed and nodded. ''Me and everybody else. I'd been trying to get him to notice me for a long time. Join the crowd, Ellyn, I used to tell myself. I knew he was like a handsome moth flitting around all the girls, but I didn't care. I was willing to wait my turn. It wasn't easy. When he cooled it with Beth, I thought maybe he'd—''

"Beth Scott?"

Ellyn blew her nose in a tissue that Curtis had offered. "They used to make out in the therapy rooms at night. Beth had a key and I saw them several times slipping in and out."

"When was this?"

"Last spring . . . before she went on her annual vacation to visit her grandparents. She and Larry never got it put together again after she came back. I don't know why they cooled it, but I was glad."

Curtis grabbed the sheet of notes that he'd taken from Beth's personnel folder. Her grandparents were listed as next of kin, Timbuck, Texas. Her yearly physical exam had been routine for a young woman in her twenties, but he had noted that it was over a year old. No family physician had been listed. Only one reference, three years old, from a teacher at Timbuck High School. The only other notation he had taken from the file was a reprimand for Beth's having been late returning from last year's May vacation.

Curtis wasn't even aware of Ellyn's leaving as he grabbed the phone and dialed long distance. The phone rang and rang before a woman answered in a cracking voice, "Hold yer horses, I'm a-comin'."

Curtis forced a relaxed chuckle into his voice. "Sorry to bother you, Mrs. Scott," he said easily, as his mind raced to find the right approach. He knew that if he said the wrong thing, she'd hang up on him in short order. "I'm a friend of Beth's."

She snorted. "One of them fly-by-night guys, no doubt. She never did have the sense of a bedbug when it came to men."

"I didn't mean we were close friends...not that way. I guess you could say I'm kind of her boss. You see, Beth's in line for an advancement...more money... better job," he lied.

"Whatcha calling me for?" she asked suspiciously.

"Well, Beth's a hard worker, but there seems to be something holding her back. She doesn't talk about herself, and I want to help her get ahead. I'm afraid there's some problem because she was late getting back from last year's vacation."

"Hell's bells! Whatcha expect the youngun to do? Get out of that smashed car and take the next train out of town?"

Curtis felt an electric shock go through him. "Beth was in a car wreck?"

"You're damn tootin', she was. Some drunk ran smack into her. Almost got her head smashed like a ripe melon."

"Was she alone? Was there a child with her?" Curtis's breathless expectation was short-lived.

"Child? Are you daffy? Beth doesn't have no kid."

"I know...but I thought...perhaps there was someone else in the car with her."

"Nope, she was alone, and a damn good thing she was." The voice changed. "Beth's all right, ain't she? Not having any more of them headaches? I told her she should have taken more time off—but she was worried about her job."

"How long was she in the hospital?"

"Oh, she didn't go to no hospital. We got a nice two-bed clinic here in Timbuck. Miss Addie Porter runs it. Best nurse there is. A doctor comes out from Fort Worth when he's called. Addie's the one who told me Beth had been fooling around behind the barn. I never told Beth that I knew about—" The woman broke off. "I shouldn't be running off at the mouth like this."

"I know you want to help Beth if you can," he said smoothly.

She answered sharply. "And I can best do that by keeping my mouth shut." She hung up with a bang.

Curtis shoved aside the frustrating disappointment and called information, Timbuck, Texas, for the residence of Addie Porter and the Timbuck Clinic.

The nurse wasn't at home, but a pleasant voice informed him that Miss Porter was in her office at the clinic.

She answered with a pleasant, "Hello. Addie Porter here."

Curtis let the urgency of his call come through each word as he identified himself and related as succinctly as possible the events that had led up to his call. He described the psychiatric profile of the woman they sought. "Miss Porter, do you have any reason to believe that Beth Scott might be suffering from maternal frustrations? It's very important. An innocent woman's life may hang in the balance."

Her answer was sure and unadorned. "Yes, it's quite possible.

Twelve hours after her automobile accident, Beth Scott had suffered a miscarriage.

Chapter Nineteen

When Gail floated upward into consciousness again, she felt a vibrating movement like the gentle rocking of an unseen hand. It was several minutes before she identified the roar of a car's engine. She struggled to orient herself as she lay on her back with a light blanket covering her from head to foot. She was in a moving car. *"A good day for a drive."*

Jagged bits of memory surfaced like flotsam in murky waters. The house. The crib. Beth! When she tried to wiggle her toes no sensation of movement was registered in her brain. Whatever had been in the hypodermic had paralyzed her. She concentrated on trying to turn her head to one side, refusing to believe that her muscles would not respond if she were determined enough.

She lost track of time, but she felt triumphant when she had wiggled her head back and forth enough to dislodge the wool blanket from her eyes. She was stretched out on the floor behind the front seat of a car. The windows were coated with snow but she could tell from the pitch that the car and the way her ears popped that it was climbing into higher elevations.

Why was Beth taking her into the mountains? From time to time the wheels seemed to slip as if trying to find purchase on a snow-covered road. She could hear other cars, so they must be on a highway, she reasoned.

Gail struggled for some idea of what Beth might be planning—and failed. When the car slowed to a stop, she bit her lip to stifle a cry of terror. What was going to happen now? She was able to lift her head for a few brief seconds before letting it fall back helplessly. The blanket remained over the lower half of her face and her arms were too weak to push it off. She closed her eyes and waited, expecting Beth to pull her out of the car like a limp sack.

Nothing happened. The car didn't move. Gail couldn't hear anything except the idling motor and the soft sweep of snow against the car. Gradually a faint echo of voices reached her. Then she heard Beth rolling down her window. "What is it, Officer? Is the road blocked?"

"No, but chains are required. Sorry, ma'am, but I'm going to have to ask you to put them on."

"It isn't snowing very hard," Beth protested. "Just a couple of inches on the ground."

"I know, but there's solid ice underneath."

"I have good tires."

"Not good enough for these snow-packed roads. No exceptions, ma'am. If you want to wait, someone will give you a hand...."

From the moment Gail had realized that rescue was a miraculous few feet away, she tried to force a loud cry through her lips, but the croaking sound that came from her mouth was muffled by the blanket that still lay over the bottom half of her face. She strained to make herself heard. If only the officer would look in the back. *Please... please.* Desperation brought hot tears into her eyes and she lifted her head higher this time. Her scalp was beginning to tingle as if her sensory and motor nerves were beginning to function again. The blanket was slowly edging down as she moved her mouth—but it was too late.

Beth had rolled up her window and Gail heard the crunch of footsteps go by the car.

No, come back... come back.

A moment later, Beth got out of the car and Gail heard her rummaging in the trunk. There was still hope, Gail thought, refusing to give in to the horrible truth that with dozens of people stopped on the highway putting on chains, no one would know that she was lying helpless in a murderer's car.

If only someone would clear off one of the windows and look inside... If only Beth would do something suspicious... If only someone would open the back door. Given a little more time, her body would begin to function again. Already her cries seemed louder in her ears. It was impossible that someone wouldn't hear her. Someone passing by the car. Someone helping with the chains. *Anyone, please!*

THE WHEELS on Curtis's car squealed hotly as he took a corner a block from the address he had copied from Beth's file. Curtis had been put through to Lamont at the police station and had poured out the information on Beth. The detective had snapped, "What's her address? I'll get a car there right away."

Curtis read the address he'd copied off her file.

"You stay out of sight. Let my men handle it. I'll be there as soon as I can."

The address was one in a western suburb of Denver called Lakewood, and the snow was heavier as Curtis approached the foothills. Lowering storm clouds had sacked the sun and cars were driving with their lights on. Curtis hunched forward over the steering wheel, his heartbeat racing wildly as his anxiety mounted. He almost missed the apartment building because it was set back from the street, sandwiched between a Royal Pizzeria and a Wash-Spin launderette. He felt a spurt of relief when he saw that a police car was already parked in a driveway at the side of the building.

He squealed to a stop in front of the Pizzeria and waited for about sixty seconds in the car before the pressure became too great. Ignoring Lamont's orders to stay out of sight, he reached the front of the apartment building just as two police officers came out the front door and Lamont's car roared into the driveway behind the patrol car.

The small man was out of the car like a bullet. Curtis's heart sank when the officers began shaking their heads before the detective reached them.

"No Beth Scott here, Lieutenant," one of them told him. "Landlord said she moved out about a year ago."

Curtis couldn't believe it. There had been a P.O. Box number in Beth's file and this address. Apparently her mail had continued to go to the post office box and she hadn't bothered to change her residence address in her personnel file.

"Landlord says her grandparents bought her a house...."

"Address?" barked Lamont.

"He doesn't know exactly. But he thinks it's in Golden somewhere."

"Golden?" Curtis swore. Golden was a small town to the west of Denver, right against the foothills, about fifteen miles away.

The lieutenant headed back to his car and Curtis followed him. A young officer, Hawkins, was slipping into the driver's seat.

"I'm going with you," said Curtis, and he climbed into the back seat of the car before either officer could object. His mind whirled like a threshing machine. There had to be a way to find the correct address—and soon. "If she bought a house, there have to be records," he said, thinking aloud.

"Exactly." Lamont reached for his intercom and began barking orders.

Curtis's heart sank when he remembered that it was Saturday. How much precious time would it take to find someone who would open up the necessary files?

GAIL LOST TRACK of the time they were stopped at the roadblock. It could have been ten minutes or an hour and ten minutes. As far as she was concerned, the progression of time was marked by the almost imperceptible return of normal sensations to her extremities. Her toes began to tingle, her skin on the calves of her legs contracted like dead tissue coming to life and the tips of her fingers prickled. In spite of the return of sensation, movement was still so labored as to be nonexistent. She could not right herself, or use her arms to throw off the blanket that covered her body. Her voice was hoarse and grew more feeble as she continued to cry for help.

Beth got back in the front seat, and the car began to move forward. Disappointment that her chance was gone brought hot tears flooding into Gail's eyes. They had passed through a roadblock with state patrol officers and dozens of other people around without anyone coming to her aid. She knew then that if she were to survive, it would have to be with her own wits. The drug was wearing off—she knew that. She was able to clench her right hand now and could feel those muscles contracting.

With the same dedication she'd given to her physical therapy exercises, Gail began to mentally tighten muscles in her arms and legs. At first, nothing happened, but little by little the strength that had been there began to come back.

Her mind raced ahead. Even at her best, she was no match for Beth's muscular physique. Whatever Beth had planned for her she'd carried it out easily and efficiently—the way she'd accomplished everything else. How diabolically clever she must have been setting up Sherrie and Wilhite's deaths to look like suicides. There was no doubt now in Gail's mind that they had been murdered.

And what about Larry? The night of the party, Beth must have been the one who left the building with him. Gail never connected Beth with the handsome flirt, but there must have been something between them for Beth to run him over. But what about Scuffy? Why would Beth leave her for dead stuffed in a cupboard? *Because she's psychotic.* The truth did nothing to alleviate a bone-shaking fear that nothing she could do would stop Beth from carrying out her vendetta.

Gail was rocked back and forth with the motion of the car as it traveled a twisting road. At last she was able to raise herself on one arm into an almost sitting position. Breath caught in her throat. A pair of eyes stared at her from the back seat.

Before Gail could bring the face into focus, the car gave an abrupt lurch. Gail fell back on the floor. She gasped in surprise when something tumbled off the seat onto her chest. Gail put her hands on it. A hysterical sob swept up into her throat. She was holding a baby doll.

LIEUTENANT LAMONT wrote down the address as a clerk in the public service company gave it to him over the car phone.

"We'll be there in five minutes," he assured Curtis. "But it could be a false lead," he warned. "Sometimes the most promising evidence adds up to a wrong answer."

"We don't have time for any wrong answers," Curtis answered grimly. He was positive that where they found Beth Scott, they would find Gail.

The address was just outside Golden's city limits. A dirt road led to a small two-story wooden house, sitting off the main road all by itself. Several dilapidated sheds and a chicken house stood at the back of the property.

Chickens. Eggs. Rotten eggs. Chicken guts.

Curtis was out of the car before either of the officers, and if he'd had any kind of weapon, he might have lost his head and rushed into the house ahead of them. Never in his life had he wanted a gun in his hand as much as he did at that moment.

Curtis went with Lamont to the front door, and Hawkins scooted around the house to the back. The front steps were covered with a blanket of virgin snow—no footprints. Lamont opened a sagging screen door and tried the front knob.

It turned.

He motioned Curtis to one side of the door and he stood on the other. He counted to ten, giving Hawkins time to get in place, and then shouted, "Police!"

In one quick movement, he shoved the door open and went through with his gun readied for firing.

Silence.

Lamont cautiously crossed the small hall and entered an adjoining living room with Curtis only a step behind him. A small television, faded couch and scarred coffee table matched the secondhand look of a couple of chairs and small tables.

Hawkins came through from the kitchen. "Nothing."

"Check the garage and outbuildings," Lamont ordered. "I'll have a look upstairs."

With his gun drawn, the lieutenant slowly mounted the stairs with Curtis behind him. About five steps from the top, he stopped. The policeman's eyes were focused on bright splotches staining the rug, and when Curtis saw the bloodstains he fought back a driving need to shout, Gail . . . Gail!

Lamont's eyes warned him to keep silent.

Curtis swallowed hard and nodded.

The detective moved quickly. The doors to a small bathroom and bedroom stood open. Both rooms were empty. Lamont gave a warning nod of his head toward the closed door at the end of the hall.

Curtis's chest was so tight that he could hardly breathe. The brooding silence in the house tore at his nerves. Every moment that passed was an excruciating eternity. He wanted to scream at Lamont to hurry as the policeman stopped in front of the door and slowly turned the knob. He leveled his gun as he flung the door open.

Both men were inside the room in an instant. The horror of a twisted mind venting itself was everywhere. Curtis's stomach turned over. A dizzying array of baby pictures covered all the walls; stuffed animals stared down with glassy eyes from crowded shelves; stacks of unopened diapers and unworn baby clothes littered tables and baby furniture; the sweet smell of baby powder and lotion was sickening. *A woman with maternal frustrations.*

Then a jagged cry caught in Curtis's throat. In the corner of the room, behind a crib, lay several pieces of clothesline cord and Gail's crumpled pale blue coat.

Chapter Twenty

In spite of the building anxiety, Curtis had clung to the belief that they would find Gail unharmed, but as he looked at the discarded rope and Gail's coat, the worst scenario possible leaped forward in his mind. The woman had brought Gail to this room, tied her up and then— His mind maliciously supplied the rest of the horror. *No!* With every ounce of will, he refused to believe that they had come too late.

Lamont knelt down beside the coat that Curtis positively identified as belonging to Gail. He pointed at a few dark splotches on the floor. "Dried blood...not much of it, though."

Curtis knew that observation was double-edged. He chose to believe it meant that Gail hadn't been seriously harmed—not that a dead person doesn't bleed much.

Lamont stood up as Hawkins came in the room. "What'd you find?"

"Nothing, sir. Garage is empty...door left open... and fresh tracks in the driveway. Didn't see any signs of footprints in the yard...or fresh digging."

The detective swung around to Curtis. "What kind of car does Scott drive?"

Curtis tried desperately to retrieve some memory of Beth's getting out of her car at Crestview. He drew a blank. "I don't know. I don't think I ever saw Beth in the parking lot, arriving or leaving. The only time I ever noticed her was in the therapy room." Curtis froze. "The accident with the therapy tank! No accident at all. She planned it all. How could I have been so stupid as not to see it?"

"Because hindsight is always twenty-twenty. Come on. The licensing bureau will probably give the info on the car, but it'll take time."

Time is what we don't have, finished Curtis, cursing himself. He'd never paid any attention to what kind of car anybody else drove, not like— His head jerked up. "Myra. My secretary knows what kind of car everybody drives. She's very conscious about that kind of thing."

"Call her."

"There's a wall phone in the kitchen," said Hawkins. "I'll use the car phone. Driver registration and license bureau, right, sir?" asked the young officer.

"Tell them it's an emergency."

Curtis found the phone and dialed Myra's number and waited while it rang and rang. *Come on... come on...* On the eighth ring, Myra's sleepy voice answered, "Hello?"

"Myra, it's Curtis," he said briskly, as if they were at the office. "I need some information from you fast. Now listen carefully. What kind of car does Beth Scott drive? Make and year."

There was a dead silence on the other end.

"Myra," he barked. "Wake up and answer me!"

"I'm trying to think," she snapped back. "Give me a break. I was up all night...policemen banging on my door. What in the hell is going on?"

"Gail's missing...and we've got to find Beth Scott. Now, answer me! What kind of car does Beth drive?"

"You're not saying that Beth—"

His voice grew as hard as stone. "Answer me, Myra. *Now!*"

"No need to shout. It's an '84 or '85 Ford sedan."

"Color?" he snapped.

"Kind of a faded burgundy. But it's not her car," Myra offered smugly.

"What do you mean?"

"It's Beth's grandparents'. They're just letting her use it. She's driving around with Texas license plates."

BETH TURNED the windshield wipers on high and smiled in satisfaction as the sign she had been looking for came into view: Scenic Overlook.

She turned off the highway. A paved area on a high bluff provided a view of the surrounding area. A closed-up tourist information trailer and two small rest rooms stood in the middle of the lookout—just as she remembered. Better than any parking lot in town, she reasoned with happy satisfaction. They'd found Larry's body much too quickly...but then, she really hadn't planned to run him over that night. He'd agreed to come out to her car because she had threatened to disgrace him in front of everyone if he didn't. When she'd told him about losing Robbie, their unborn baby, he'd just laughed at her.

"You're off your rocker, honey. We haven't had anything going for a year."

"But that's when it happened. I was pregnant when I took my vacation last spring...you know, when I was gone three extra weeks?" Her lips had trembled. "I lost the baby because of a car accident. I didn't say anything when I came back...but since you're the father..."

"Hey, kiddo. You're not sticking me with any retroactive knock-up. I'm out of here." He slammed out of the car.

Beth could still hear his mocking laughter in her ears. But the last laugh was hers, she thought with satisfaction. She'd overtaken him in her car halfway across the lot. She could still see the way his arms had gone up and the horror written on his face just before she ran him over. Then she'd driven around the building, left the car parked on the other side and returned to the party. No one had noticed her absence. She had pretended to be as shocked as everyone when O'Mallory came in to report the hit-and-run.

It had been a perfect cover-up until that brat, Scuffy, had taunted her. "You liked Larry, you liked Larry. But he didn't like you." The brat had been hiding out the night of the party and overheard part of her conversation in the hall with Larry before they went outside. Fortunately, the kid didn't know how incriminating that bit of information would have been if it had reached the right ears. Blasted little snoop, swore Beth. When the brat had taken off in the electric wheelchair, it'd been pure luck that she'd found her first.

Beth smiled, remembering how she had caught up with Scuffy at Richards's front step. Her only mistake was not making sure the kid was dead before she stuffed her in the wardrobe. Beth frowned. That was a piece of unfinished business she'd have to take care of before the brat came out of her coma.

At the moment, Gail Richards was the one who must pay for her evil deeds. Beth was glad it was snowing. Perfect. Everything would be covered nicely. A foot of snow would lie on top of Gail's snowy grave before the storm moved on, she thought with satisfaction. And who knew how long it would be before a snowplow came along to discover that justice had been done.

GAIL KNEW that the drug had worn off because every inch of her body was racked with pain. Even though she could move her legs, she had to bite her lip to keep from crying out. The baby doll still lay on her chest, and Gail was steeling herself to sit up when the car stopped.

The driver's door flew open and Beth came around to open the back door at Gail's head. Grasping Gail's arms in an iron grip, she pulled Gail out of the car headfirst and dragged her across the snowy ground. The blanket of cold snow blessedly numbed Gail's pain.

The steady hum of the engine broke the silence of softly falling snow and bright headlights speared the white blanket in front of the car. Gail's thinly clad body was covered with snow when Beth dropped her a few feet in front of the car. Then Beth turned back to the car, and Gail knew her life was measured in seconds.

Dear God, no! She lacked any kind of weapon. Nothing she could say to Beth now would have any effect on her twisted mind. She didn't have the strength to get up and run. And yet the idea of lying passively in the snow waiting for car wheels to crush her was a defeat Gail would not suffer. She would try to crawl away... if only for a few feet before the end came.

She started to move and realized then that she still had the baby doll grasped to her chest. She almost shoved it away from her when an intuitive flash stopped her. *Use the woman's madness.*

Gail forced a desperate cry from her lungs as she struggled to sit up. "Beth! Beth! Your baby." She held the doll up in the air. "Here's your baby."

Through waves of softly falling snowflakes Gail could see that Beth was hesitating beside the open door. The car was still running. Would she get in and shut the door—or would she come back?

"The baby wants his mommy." Gail cried loudly. "Mommy! Mommy!" And she shook the doll as viciously as she could and made loud baby cries.

Beth came running back. "No. No. Stop. Stop!"

With strength born out of desperation, Gail threw the doll as far as she could. The doll turned over in the air, hit the edge of an embankment and slid down a nearby snow-covered slope.

Beth gave an anguished cry and ran after it.

Gail couldn't see how far the doll had slipped down the hill, but even before Beth disappeared over the rim, Gail was on her knees and then her legs as she staggered wildly toward the car.

She almost made it and then her feet slipped out from under her just as she reached the open car door.

Beth came up over the edge of the hill, the snow-covered doll in her arms. With a wild cry, she ran full speed toward the car.

Gail grabbed the door handle and pulled herself up. Grasping the steering wheel, she hauled herself into the front seat. She pulled the door shut, shoved the lock down in place only seconds before Beth's hand touched the outside door handle.

Gail's breath came in strangled breaths. Her head fell forward and she struggled to keep from fainting. Beth screeched and banged on the window with such force that the glass threatened to shatter in a thousand pieces.

Gail raised her head, and a hurricane pounded and thrashed inside her skull. Beth screeched at her and then darted around the back of the car as if she remembered that the back door on the passenger's side was unlocked.

The car was still running and Gail's trembling hand found the gearshift. Her snow-covered body shivered uncontrollably as one foot touched the gas pedal.

Beth jerked open the back door.

Catching her lower lip in her teeth, Gail shoved the gear into Drive and jammed down on the gas.

The sudden acceleration caused the tires to spin without traction. The car failed to move forward.

With a cry of triumph, Beth was halfway in the back seat when the car suddenly lunged forward and threw her off balance. She managed to hold on to the door frame for several seconds before it was jerked out of her hand. She fell backward and tumbled out of sight as the car took off.

A blur of sweeping headlights and slanting snowfall blinded Gail as the car surged ahead. Disoriented, she strained her eyes, trying to make some sense of where she was. She swerved away from a guardrail and didn't see the tourist information trailer until it rose up in front of her.

She tried to brake. The car sailed forward like a sled. It plowed into the side of the trailer. Walls of wood and plaster crumpled like crackers, burying the car's hood in the debris while the rest of it stuck out unscathed. Gail was stunned by the impact.

Beth was right there and she reached through a broken window on the passenger side and unlocked the front door. Her eyes burned like hot coals and her expression was one of maniacal glee as she reached across the seat.

She sank her fingers into Gail's flesh as she dragged her out of the car once more. This time she pulled her through the snow toward the edge of the overlook. Beyond the low railing the earth fell away thousands of feet. Beth pulled Gail to her feet and balanced her inert body against the guardrail as she prepared to throw her over the side. An expression akin to someone making a sacrifice crossed Beth's face. Her lips moved with inaudible muttering and a luminous glow touched her eyes as snowflakes caught on her eyelashes and covered her hair.

"Don't do this, Beth," pleaded Gail weakly.

Beth looked into Gail's face, and for a moment a flicker of regret flickered. "It's for Robbie," she said sadly.

At that moment, the trailer behind them caught fire with a burst of flame that shot into the sky. For a grotesque moment, orange and red light played across Beth's face as she turned her head toward the fire.

Later Gail couldn't sort out all the things that happened in a split second. An explosion shook the ground. Flying wood and metal filled the air. A deadly shower of missiles rained like arrows in their direction.

Beth gave an earsplitting scream and her hands suddenly fell away from Gail. For a moment Gail couldn't understand what had happened. Then she saw in horror that something was embedded in the back of Beth's skull. In slow motion, she fell forward over the railing and disappeared from view.

CURTIS SAT RIGIDLY in the police car traveling at top speed west on Interstate 70. With flashing lights, Officer Hawkins passed slow traffic while Lamont kept his ears glued to the crackling shortwave. The All Points Bulletin that Lamont had put out on Beth's car had miraculously brought quick response from an officer working a roadblock on Interstate 70. He remembered the car and Texas license plates because the woman driver had given him a bad time.

"She passed through about a couple of hours ago," he told the detective. "Sorry I didn't know earlier. I would have stopped her."

Every mile Curtis berated himself for not having moved faster. He agonized over the time he'd spent on

Roberta, Ellyn and Myra. If only he'd started with Beth...called her grandparents first thing. At every turn, he could have cut minutes...even hours off the time it had taken to bring them to this point in the pursuit.

Lamont sat hunched in the front seat. He knew there were hundreds of places a car could turn off the highway. The only hope was that the woman's car might have run into trouble. If she had been detained in a line of stalled vehicles or spun out herself, there was a chance they could catch up to her. She wouldn't be able to get back to the city without being detained—but that might be too late. He sighed. *Maybe it was already too late.* Sometimes he hated his job.

The report of a tourist trailer on fire came through on the shortwave when they were about a mile from the scenic overlook. Some transients trying to get out of the weather, thought Lamont with little interest. No vacant trailer or cabin was safe with the weather like this.

"Shall we check it out?" asked Hawkins.

Lamont shook his head. "Let one of the state patrolmen make the report. We can't let the woman get any more of a lead. I wonder where in blazes she's going."

A short distance from the fire, Curtis saw the bright glow through his side window. A weird glow was reflected in the sky and the luminous snow-covered ground. Flames shot into the air, spewing multicolored sparks like confetti. As he stared at the scene, Gail's face formed clearly in the window glass. His heart jumped. Without analyzing the impression, Curtis jerked forward in his seat.

"Stop at the fire."

"We don't have time—"

"Either stop—or let me out."

Lamont turned and looked at Curtis. The detective had followed a few hunches of his own from time to time. He nodded to Hawkins. "All right. We'll take a quick look."

Heat radiated from the burning trailer and rest rooms as they parked and stepped out of the car. Lamont let out an explosive breath. "There's a car burning up with the trailer."

The frame was barely visible. No way of knowing what kind of car . . . or who it belonged to. But Curtis knew. They had found Beth Scott's car.

"Gail! Gail!" Curtis started yelling. He spun around, searching with his eyes in every direction.

"Easy, son." Lamont grabbed his arm. "If she's in that car, she can't hear you."

Curtis jerked away from Lamont. "Gail . . . Gail."

The answering cry was faint, but he had heard it. He ran toward the edge of the bluff. At first he didn't see her because she was just a snow-covered mound blending in with the railing posts.

"Gail . . . Gail. Where are you?"

No answer.

Then she wavered to her knees and fell forward on her face. He threw himself toward her and gathered her into his arms, pressing his face against hers with tearful relief. "Dear God, you're all right."

For an answer, she raised her arms and locked them firmly around his neck.

Chapter Twenty-One

The grass was green, daffodils bloomed along the walk and June sunlight came through the dining room windows. A three-tier wedding cake sparkled in the middle of the table, and sugared pink flowers decorated the white icing, except on one side where three were missing.

"Scuffy, you leave the cake alone!" ordered Angie. "I saw you sneaking in here." Then Angie widened her eyes as she stared at the top of the cake. "Where are the bride and groom dolls?"

The freckle-faced little girl scowled. "I don't know."

"Scuffy." Angie put her hands on her hips.

Reluctantly Scuffy brought her arm around from behind her back and handed the cake decoration back to Angie. "I just wanted to look at them," she said defiantly.

After Gail and Curtis cut the cake and were moving among the small gathering of wedding guests, Angie told Gail what had happened. "Scuffy's back to normal, all right."

Both Gail and Curtis laughed. "We'd better inventory all the gifts before she squirrels half of them away," said Curtis.

"There are a few more that you haven't opened. This one came by special delivery."

Gail looked at the package in Angie's hands, and for a moment the old anxiety was back. Her face paled. Her hand felt sweaty against the ecru lace of her wedding gown. Then she looked up at Curtis and the shadows disappeared. His loving presence was all she needed to put the past beyond her.

"Go ahead, darling, open it," he urged. His dark blue eyes said, *It's all right . . . it's all right.*

Gail's fingers trembled at first, and then grew steady as she pulled back the wrapping paper from the box.

"My goodness, who sent that?" breathed Angie in awe.

Gail raised her eyes to Curtis. "My husband." She blushed as she held up a sheer nightgown shimmering with all the colors of the rainbow.

"Thank you." She knew that his purpose in sending the gift was to chase away any lingering apprehensions.

"Let's get out of here," he whispered. Their suitcases were packed and ready for a three-week honeymoon in Bermuda.

Angie laughed and winked at Tony as they slipped out of the room. At the bottom step, Curtis swept her up in his arms.

"I can walk up by myself," she protested.

He said gently, "I know you can...but I want to carry you." His eyes searched her face.

A smile eased into the corner of her lips. "I'd like that," she said, relaxing and leaned her head against his chest.